A Violet

Night

Where even the best of us hav   ...oments...

by

B. Kaitlyn

A Violet Night

© COPYRIGHT 2022 BRITTANY VALLEROY – ALL RIGHTS RESEVERED.

A Violet Night

Table of Contents

Table of Contents

A Violet Night

A Story 13 Years In The Making...

<u>Chapter 1.)</u>

Rory opened his eyes to a warm burning beam of light shining through his cracked window. The dust glistened in the one lonely beam of sun floating across the air gently swaying back and forth. The cool breeze grazed his skin gently, creating shivers as it danced up his left arm. He stretched his long body and glanced to his side and saw that Visha was still fast asleep, one leg hanging off of the bed. He rubbed his eyes and groaned "Oh shit!". Sliding himself out of bed and throwing his clothes on as fast as he could. He knew that he could not be late again for morning line up. He rinsed his mouth out with some left over water next to the bed, then carefully placing her leg back into the bed and back underneath the covers.

He shut the door behind him it bounced back open, the wooden frame was swollen again. His eye twitched, as he slammed it the second time. Tucking his shirt into his pants as he raced down the stone hallway as fast as he could. Tripping on the long velvet red rug with the gold tassels he dodged all of the maids carrying their fresh linen, and water pitchers as they lurched out of his way annoyed. "Watch where you're going!" One shouted. "Late again Ri?" Another scoffed holding a door open for him. "You know it!" He shouted racing past her with a wink. She rolled her eyes as he scrambled through.

Taking the last doorway on the right Rory made his way through the kitchen and into the garden. He heard a softer unfamiliar voice talking from behind the overflowing grape vines. He continued running all the while thinking about all the things his uncle would do if he showed up late again. His mind wondered about the upcoming day.

Meanwhile his legs felt as if they were racing on top the

clouds. He tried to pace his breathing, as the air pierced his

lungs sharply like cold water. Suddenly he hit something,

not just something, but someone.

"Are you okay?!" he exclaimed helping the girl off

him "I'm so sorry-" he paused as their eyes met. "It's fine."

The girl muttered with a reassuring grin. He gave a small

smile back. He smiled up at Elda too. She slowly shook her

head at him bringing her wrinkles on her forehead down in

disappointment, but that look was nothing new. She was

always telling him to stay out of *her* kitchen ever since he

had been a boy. She loved to tell him "That it had enough

rats already."

He looked at the girl one more time, suddenly he

was at a loss for words, awkwardly he waved and laughed

before taking off again in a light jog. He looked over his

shoulder at her again nearly hitting the gate on his way out. Embarrassed by himself he picked up his pace.

Finally, he made it to the morning line up taking his place next to Lee in line; just in time as the captain was getting to his row of the guards. Rory huffed trying to regain his breath. "Maybe you were promoted to guard duties to soon nephew." The captain said looking down at him harshly. "No sir. Sorry sir." He said standing up straighter, holding his breath so no one could hear his loud panting. Lee tried to contain his laughter at the captain shot him a stern look. His chuckles became an empty look off in front of him as he tried to transition into a fake cough.

Once they endured their morning run down they were given their post to patrol. Rory & Lee were given stable duty for their behavior, and as boring as that was it gave them a chance to catch up since they had last seen each other the night before at the tavern in town.

A Violet Night

"Where were you? Wait no, don't tell me you were with Visha again." Lee said taunting him. "She's really not that bad" He played it off. "After all I'm sure she uh- she fills your void." Lee said raising an eyebrow, "You do know if you keep bringing her home from the brothel like that you're bound to end up with her in real life too." He made a cradling motion with his arms. Rory rolled his eyes "She knows it's just casual. Nothing romantic about it." "Does she really?" Lee asked smugly. He gave his friend a shove in the arm "She's just nice to talk to.. it's not even like that most nights.". Lee raised his eyebrows "Most nights.." he said with a laugh.

Rory grabbed a shovel and began to drift into his thoughts, still listening as Lee's voice became muffled in his lecture. He sat down. At this time could not think about Visha, all he had on his mind was the green-eyed girl he had bumped into in the garden, and the way her black wavy hair hung around her shoulders. He could still smell her perfume through his mind. Lavender? Mixed with Honey or maybe vanilla? He began to wonder why he hadn't seen her before. Maybe she was one of the kings visiting guest, but then why would she be with Elda in the garden?

His concentration was broken when one of the horses nudged him on the back trying to get to the hay he was sitting on. He stood up petting the muzzle of the large beast. "Where is your head at?" Lee asked confused, "I've been talking to you this entire time Ri. Meanwhile you've just been sitting there with this same damn dumb expression on your face.".

"Heh, I uh- I ran into this girl today." He said still staring off. "Ri, you run into a lot of girls. Actually run into." He said sarcastically making a thrusting motion with his hips. "No. I physically ran into a girl today, I actually knocked her off her feet. No pun intended." Before Lee could say anything else inappropriate he kept talking "She was with Elda, I think she's going to start working in the kitchen?".

Lee completely ignoring Rory asked, "I sure do love that woman, momma Elda… Hey, do you think if I asked her, she would make us those fruit pastries like she did that one time when we were boys out there picking fruit from the vineyard?". Rory shrugged his shoulders as the memories flooded back to him of the two then small boys racing to see who could fill up their baskets the fastest "You'll probably have to bribe her with something, you know they've been preparing all week for that suiters ball for the princess.". "So you think my good looks wouldn't be enough to persuade her?" He said devilishly playing with his short patchy beard. "Now you know you're ugly right?" Rory scoffed playfully. "It could be worse I could look like you." He snarked back.

Rory opened his mouth to speak, "Guerrero." His uncles voice rang out like thunder as he turned the side of the stable. Rory straightened up and was now wide eyed looking at his captain. "Well boy, time to regain my respect. Kings orders are to escort the princess and his niece around the kingdom ground. Since I have somewhere to be I am trusting that you will take care of the matter.". "That's wonderful news!" Lee smiled. "No. No. Not you Gomez. I need you here today." The captain said handing Lee the shovel out of Rory's hand and nodding towards the piles a feces in the pin. Lee shot Rory a look. Rory laughed and mouthed "Have fun.". Lee groaned and pulled the shovel from his hand, dropping it the second it hit his fingertips.

The captain nodded at Rory "Don't screw this up kid." He nodded back at him assuring. "I'll try my best not too" He said smugly. "Oh, one more thing" He said turning back around to his nephew. His mouth came open and then he smiled "Never mind. I'm sure you'll figure out her when you meet her.".

"Must be nice to have an uncle in command." Lee said enviously. "Don't you have a job to do?" Rory said pointing around with his eyes. Lee clicked his tongue annoyed "Go. Before I fling this at you." He said holding a scoop of feces as flies swarmed him.

The air was thick and hot now approaching midday. He slowly made his way back up to the garden and back through the long stone hallway. As he walked the walls began to take a turn for the brighter, more colors, adding paintings of the royal family, all poised and posed the queen with her daughters their long dirty blonde hair pinned up clutching onto each other, the king with his empty yet empty look in his eyes, and long curtains that draped to the floor. He made his way to the foyer he saw a small, pale blonde girl sitting on the bench frowning at him. "Great." He whispered preparing himself forcing a half fake smile.

A Violet Night

He stood there for a moment waiting, he bowed before the princess on the bench. She looked passed him. He heard quiet footsteps from the North hallway the same girl he had bumped into in the garden entered the room. "How long where you going to keep me waiting here cousin?" She stood up coldly walking passed Rory fanning herself. "Nice to see you again as well." She came up to her and gave her a small pitiful hug. She turned to Rory whose mouth was now wide open in confusion, "Just wanted to bump into me again?" The girl asked tilting her head with a smirk. His head was turning with words to say but his head could not keep up with what he wanted to say.

A Violet Night

Chapter 2.)

"Violet, now come on.. You know you can't be caught down here again!" Elda said judgingly shewing her towards the door with her flour covered hands. Violet rolled her eyes and took an apple out of the fruit bowl "This is the kitchen. Where food is kept, and I'm hungry. I am more than capable of getting my own food. Besides you know as well as I do by the time I've told someone to fetch me an apple it will flow through six other mouths, and they'll come back with a pear.". Elda smiled at her dusting her frail wrinkled hands off on her apron "Then while you're here help me collect some of the fruit from the garden for these pies.". She slid a wicker basket across the rugged countertop. "It is my party after all. I suppose I could help you gather supplies." She said with a smile setting her freshly bitten into apple down, grabbing the basket and placing it to the middle of her stomach. Violet rushed ahead of Elda to hold the door open for her. "Always good to see those manners I taught you are still in there." She said with a grin.

Together they headed outside, Violet looked around at the vas spread of green leafy trees overflowing with many fruit. The flowers and herbs growing wildly alongside of the wall, and finally her favorite the grape vines. they were divided into two rows. One for wine and the other for eating.

She always admired how they grew, how they twisted and warped around each other. She snuck a grape into her mouth. "In the basket not your mouth." Elda said without turning around to look at her. Violet never understood how she was so good at that. She gave a grin then continued to walk around the vines plucking the juiciest of fruits for Elda's pastries and pies. Tracing them with her fingertips feeling the different textures on their skins. Violet let out a sigh.

"My dear, what is the matter today?" Elda asked picking a bright red tomato from the vine. Violet paused "I don't know anymore. I have grown tired of this life we live day in and day out.".

As swift as a jolt of lightning Violet was being knocked down to the ground, by a force that came onto her body as if she had struck a solid stone wall. It knocked the wind out of her lungs.

She looked up at the man who knocked her to the ground as she tried to regain her breath. He grabbed her arm firmly without applying too much pressure and yanked her to her feet as if she was weightless. "Are you okay?" the man asked rushed slowly letting go of her. "I'm so sorry-" Violet met his gaze, and in that split moment it felt like the very pit of her stomach was on fire. "It's fine" she said with a small grin. He smiled back at her and continued running out of the garden. She giggled to herself as his stumbled looking back at her.

"What a strange, and obnoxious man." Violet cocked her head to the side and said to Elda. "Hmm. Oh Rory?" she replied turning back to the vines. "How do you know who he is?" Violet asked. "Honey, I know everyone and their granddaddy around this place.. In fact I helped take care of yours." She chuckled "He is among one of your fathers new many guards. His family has served yours for generations... If you ever went to your fathers' meetings instead of sneaking off you'd know that.". Violet rolled her eyes. "You've known his Uncle all your life. Captain Gaurrero.". "Really?" Violet said with an off high pitch tone.

A Violet Night

"So what time Harriet coming this afternoon?" Elda asked to change to subject. Violet eyes widened she had nearly forgotten about Harriet coming to spend the week with her. "Shit, like now." Violet said loudly "Language! Violet you are still a lady." Elda scolded. She gave Elda a kiss on the cheek and took off down the hallway setting her basket on the countertop as she went.

She dreaded this week out of the year more than any other. Seven days out of the year her father and her uncle try to reconnect by forcing their daughters to spend time together. Up until five years ago Harriet would accompany her time with her sister Ann for many weeks out of the year. Sometimes for no occasion at all.

Until Ann *'mysteriously'* drowned in the creek. Ann was only 20 years old. A true tragedy to this world. She was the light at the end of the tunnel for everyone who ever met her. Her voice was calm even when she was mad and with such a soothing tone you would soon forget all your worries and anxieties.

Violet still thinks of that dreadful day they heard the news of her mangled body found washed up on the rocks. The image of her mother hitting her knees followed by an unmatched scream that escaped her lips, followed by silent sobbing into her father's arms… A scream of true pain that haunts her dreams making her wake up with her heart racing out of her chest to this day. They lost their daughter that day, but Violet lost her best friend.

Now, Ann and Harriet could have passed for sisters. The two were almost identical in every way. Ann's hair was so light brown it was almost blonde not a wave or a curl in it. While Harriet's hair was the color of the sun, so blonde it was almost white at times in the summer months. Not a freckle or a mole on either ones' body that you could see. The boldest blue topaz eyes that would melt the thickest stone, both very tall in size if they got caught in a windstorm they would probably blow away as Elda liked to say. The pair wore the brightest of colors, both beyond poised truly beautiful in all of their parents eyes. They always did have to be the center of attention. More so Harriet then her sister. No, Ann was very humble. She did not have her nose stuck very high to the sky. She balanced her cousin out to a tolerable level.

Violet was number 3 of her mother and fathers children. After Ann, her mother gave birth to a baby boy named Akiva. Born with black curly hair and glimmering blue-green eyes. But tragically the Gods did not let him live long enough see his first birthday. His body just shut down one night and did not awake with the suns rise. Soon enough their tears became smiles as they soon found out they were pregnant again, hoping for another son, an heir to the throne Violet was born.

I suppose that's why Ann was always her mother and fathers favorite. Violet just as her brother before her had hair the darkest shade of black. She had freckles that flowed across the bridge of her nose and her cheek bones like the weeds overflowing a field, eyes so green they would make an emerald jealous (or cat eyes as Elda referred to them.). She had olive skin that stayed tan all year round. She was short in size unlike the rest of her family. Her Mother and Father always told her that the Gods where playing a sickening joke on them for making her in the likeness of her brother.

She was only one hallway away from the foyer when her father's voice stopped her in her tracks. "Violet!" he stood waiting for her against the wall, "Down with the servants again? I thought I told you-". "I know, I know. I'm not allowed to mingle with the servants." Violet cut him off "I know I'm late father. So can I just go get this over with already?". He nodded disappointedly at her "We will talk about this more later. Try and be nicer to her this time, and maybe she wouldn't act the way she does to you.".

A Violet Night

She shook her head as she walked away from him annoyed. Walking into the entrance to the foyer she couldn't believe her eyes, her palms began to feel sweaty. The guard her father forced to go with Harriet and herself was the man that had ran her down this morning. *"Just my luck."* She thought to herself,. "How long where you going to keep me waiting here cousin?" She stood up impatiently, they hugged one another. Violet turned to the guard "Just wanted to bump into me again?". She watched as his eyes grew bigger. She quickly pulled her gaze away, his strong yet soft eye contact sent a surge of warmth through her chest.

"Alright. Let's get this shit show on the road then shall we?" Violet said with a clap of her hands and the fakest smile she could possibly force on her face. Rory let out a snicker. He couldn't help himself. Harriet shot him a look, "I'm sorry, but was that humorous to you?". He quickly composed himself and opened the door that led outside. He used his hand to gesture outside. Harriet

walked ahead, "I thought it was rather amusing myself."

Violet whispered to him as she passed through. He grinned

at her meeting her eyes once again. Following her as he

shut the heavy door.

A Violet Night

Chapter 3.)

He took the lead walking in front of them to the way to the stables. All the while listening to Harriet whine about the long ride over to her uncles kingdom. "Wait here, and I'll get the horses ready." He said going into the stables. Once he was out of eyesight Violet made her way to the over to the fencing and slithered her body underneath it. She watched him as he talked to another guard. They both looked at her now on the other side of the fencing. She broke eye contact with him, it made her feel that feeling again when he looked at her. It excited her.

"What the hell are you doing?" Harriet asked confused "Now you're filthy!". Violet rolled her eyes and

started petting a black and tan horse "Who's a good girl"
Violet said scratching the horses nose as she came around
to her head.

"Whaaat are ya doin?" Rory asked confused from
the stable doors. "What does it look like I am doing? I'm
getting Lola out to ride." She stammered back as she
climbed up onto the horse. "Lola?" He asked under his
breath. Violet nodded. "We really have to ride these...
things?" Harriet whined walking out from the stable doors
using her cloth fan to escape the smell. "Any other ideas ?
Hmm.. No Perhaps, I don't know a carriage?".

"A carriage promotes wealth princess. Which in
forth promotes robbers. So it is this or walking I suppose. If
you ride you won't even have to do anything. I'll be
guiding the horse from the ground." Reassured Rory
patting the horse on the side of the neck proudly.

A Violet Night

After a grueling persuasion Harriet finally agreed to sit on the horse as long as she did not have to touch it. "Ladies… are we ready?" Rory asked a little agitated. Violet sat up from her lounging position on Lola as Rory reached up to grab the reins out of her hands. She pulled them closer to her chest. Lightly tapping her heels alongside Lola as she started a slow steady trot.

Rory watched for a split second with his hand still in the air letting her get a head start in front of them. He honestly didn't mind distancing himself from her at this point. Hoping to walk alongside quietly he set off looking back at Lee who puckered his lips and sucking in his cheeks not knowing what to say. He minded his own business and continued to sweep looking down.

Violet looked back and sighed realizing how far behind the other two really were. "We could keep going?" she joked. Lola neighed. She laughed pulling on the reigns stopping her and hopped off. "Okay, have it your way L." Violet whispered sarcastically petting Lola's mane.

She soon looked around at the trees and inhaled the fresh hot crisp air. Letting it fill her lungs to the top. This is what she longed for in her life. The great wide open. Everything was so green and alive, which filled her in the sense that she too was alive inside. She felt so comforted by the warm breeze on her neck as she pulled her long hair to the side running her fingers through it. She looked up feeling the sun rays on her cheeks.

She sat down on a bolder to take everything in all at once. Then she heard it. That distinct sound of Harriett moaning, groaning, and carrying on. She couldn't help but laugh at the expression on the guards' face. So blank and empty trying his hardest not to give her any attention. Violet couldn't think of a time where a man had treated Harriett in this way. They have always swooned over her for even a glance in their direction.

A Violet Night

"It's about time you caught up." Violet snickered at him "Thought you two had gotten lost?". "I just don't understand how you can just take off on these nasty beasts! To make it worse you just set off on your own so nonchalantly like you don't know what could happen to you alone out here." Harriett exclaimed shamefully. "Are you finished?" She asked calmly taking Lolas' reigns into her hands. Harriett stared at her for a judgmental moment "You always think I'm out to get you don't you Violet? Do you forget what happened to your sister? That could have been avoided if she hadn't been on her own!".

Violet raised her voice "She wasn't supposed to be alone Harriet! I do not think there will ever be a day I don't think about what happened to her! I am not my sister. I am not Ann.". "That's abundantly obvious that you're not." Harriett snarked. "What's that supposed to mean?" Violet asked. "I think you know exactly what I meant by that.".

"Alright. Alright. That's enough." Rory interrupted with both of his hand in the air. Both of the girls looked at him angrily. "I honestly do not want to hear any more of your awful bickering! You sound like children!". "You should bite your tongue more often, before it gets you into trouble." Harriet said coldly. Violet let out a short sigh rolling her eyes and begun to walk next to Lola.

"Stop." Rory sternly said. "Why?" Violet asked confused "The road doesn't end just because you want it too." Violet said without stopping to turning around. "You're right. The road doesn't end here, but unfortunately for you it does today" He said jogging to close the small gap in between them. He looked her in the eyes, as if to tell her again to *'turn around'*.

Violet bit the inside of her lip, "Tell me why?" "Who actually gives a shit." Harriet said annoyed. They ignored her and continued not looking at anything other than each other. "I actually don't have to explain it to you, but since you seem hell bent on this.. This is the part of the woods where even the poorest of the poor would never dare come. It's filled with all of the thieves, rapist, murders, & outcast of your families kingdom. Your father placed all of the kingdoms twisted misfits into a small collection between the city and the palace. Guarded only by his most trusted on the end closest to the castle walls. There is a path to go through safely. Had you not taken off so wildly we could have taken the safer route.". Violet continued to stare into his golden brown eyes. There was no trace of humor in his tone. Although she wanted to continue to test his limits his sincerity in his tone made it hard for her to form words from within.

"So are we leaving or are we going to all sit around and have a staring contest." Harriet said with a small, agitated laugh swatting the air in front of her own face "Because if I get bit by one more dastardly insect, I'm going to scream.".

A Violet Night

Violet looked at them both and stubbornly turned Lola around. She nodded at him reluctantly. He reached for her hand to help her back up. "I think I'll walk back, I need to stretch anyways." He hesitantly moved his hand back to his side. He proceeded back to Harriet's horse, as Violet began to walk ahead again, "If you're going to walk may you at least walk were I can see you?" He asked. Violet slid her way around Lola, so she was walking just a head of them now. "Thank you my lady." He said with a since of gravel in his voice. Violet smiled to herself keeping her eyes ahead as to not be seen.

"You have a-" Rory said pulling a leaf from Violets hair "-A leaf." He said awkwardly showing her. "It's been in there this whole time. I just wasn't sure if I could grab it out or if I should just tell you?". Violet took it from his possession and laughed showing her teeth. "Yes, thank you." She said dropping it at their feet. He smiled at her and chuckled. He placed the saddles and reigns in their rightful places wiping them down as he went.

"Violet come along we have to be going, it's almost evening." Harriet said rushing her cousin as she began her decent up the hill.

A Violet Night

Chapter 4.)

Violet looked to her right at Rory. He was so strange to her. Before today she never would have fathomed that someone would talk to her in the way he did today. In a way she found it profoundly refreshing to not have a 'yes man' in her ear.

"Why are you looking at me that way?" Rory said as he glanced at her letting out a curious grin. Violet laughed embarrassed with herself. She didn't realize he had been paying attention to her "Big plans tonight?". "Yeah. I have a thing… I'll probably be roped into watching a bunch of drunken, well over dressed people take their lives for granted." He chuckled. Violet found herself feeling ignorant for a second, how could she ask him that kind of a question? She felt her face get hot.

He looked away from her to stop laughing and looked back at her with a daring grin. "I did not mean to ask that in that way." Violet said embarrassed. "After all Princess.. what did you think I would be doing this evening?" He asked slyly. She shook her head "I'm sorry. I don't know exactly why I said that.". "You asked a question. Why would you be sorry for it?" He asked.

She stood there as her mind drew a blank not having an answer for him but continuing on "Well then, in that case I guess I will be seeing you there tonight then?" She watched as he began to smile tucking his tongue into the corner of his cheek "We will see.". She looked ahead to see Harriett tapping her foot, arms crossed, while staring vigorously at the two of them from the doorway. Rory thrust his right hand forward as if to tell her to go. She found herself smiling as she approached Harriet.

A Violet Night

Harriet looked at Violet with a sense of confusion and concern. "What?" Violet asked turning her smile into a frown. Harriet simply shook her head and began to walk inside "We need to start getting ready. I will help you tonight. In hopes that we could find you a suiter who can see past all of your reckless shenanigans.". She turned to the guard. He waved at her sarcastically and began on his own way. Harriet grabbed her arm pulling her alongside.

Violet couldn't help but let her mind retrace the events from that morning. Replaying in her head over, and over in a loop. She snapped herself back to reality, for now anyways she had other more 'important' things to think about, like how to make it through this ball without strangling Harriet with her own two hands. She tightened the bow on her rob walking into the privy that conjoined the bedrooms of Harriet and herself. Elda walked in behind her. She followed her to the caldron that dangled over the fireplace in the corner of the room. Bucket after bucket Violet helped Elda fill the two silver clawfoot bathtubs.

"Well, if I would have known you were going to do my job I would have just sat on down.". Elda laughed pouring the last of the water into the last tub. She took the bucket from her hands "Gets done a heck of a lot faster if someone is there to help. Besides by the time you would have done it on your own my water would have been ice cold.". Violet teased. "It's not nice to make fun of the elderly my dear, after all one day your tight perfect skin will droop just as mine does." She said smartly pinching her own cheeks with a laugh. "Touché.". Violet replied slipping out of her rob and into steamy water. "Where is little miss too good for everything?" Elda prompted pulling a stool behind the tub.

Harriet cleared her throat as she walked into the room giving Elda the evil eye. "I don't think it is polite to speak ill of someone if they are not present." Harriet spat as she dropped her rob onto to floor almost slipping as she got into the other tub. Violet splashed the water on her face to keep from laughing out loud. "I'm sorry your highness." Elda whispered. "You should be.". Harriet said rudely "Now wash my hair.". Elda sighed as she slid the stool across the black marble floor to the other tub. "Do not talk to her that way." Violet said looking over at them "You can wash yourself in here." She said looking at Elda. She smiled back at her scooting the stool back as she dried her hands "I will wait out here for you both.".

Violet scrubbed her body with a bar of soap. She sunk down into the water letting herself completely submerge underneath. She sat back up pushing her hair out of her face. Drawing her knees to her chest she found herself lost in her own little world as she watched the fire dance and crackle in the fireplace across the room.

"Vi! Let's go we have places to be and that mass of hair on your head is going to take time to dry." Harriet said breaking her concentration on the fire. She turned around to see Elda drying off Harriet's naked body "Are your hands broken dear cousin?" She asked stepping out of the large tub and grabbing a towel hanging by the fire. She began to dry herself off. "Why have all of these people if not to use them any way seem fit?" Harriet asked while Elda covered her with a new clean robe. Violet shook her head "Spoiled.". "I do not see any other way to live." Harriet said smiling back at her greedily. "I think you mean to say that you know no other way to live." Violet said putting on her old robe.

"Are your floors always this cold?" Harriet asked prancing her way to the bed to grab some stockings. Violet ignored her reaching for her undergarments. "Cremes first!" Harriet said lathering her body with a flowery smell. "Right.." Violet said going to her vanity "Here child I made this for you." Elda said reaching into her pocket. She gave it to her in her cupped hands. A small blue glass container she twisted it open. The smell of Lavender crème, and vanilla hit her nose bringing to life the visions of her sister in her head. "I know I said I would only make certain scents for each of you but, I feel like you could use a little piece of her lately.".

Violet hugged her tightly "Thank you." She whispered "Well go on. Put it on so it can dry." Elda said smiling.

"Now, what shall we put you in?" Harriet said studying over her cousin while touching all of her wardrobe "No too plump for this one." She said pushing a silk pink dress out of the way "Ah, what about this?" She asked. "Lovely." Elda said looking "You haven't had a chance to wear this one yet!" She said admiring her own work.

A Violet Night

Chapter 5.)

"How was it?" Lee asked peeling the skin off an orange. "How was what?" Rory asked. "You know.. Getting to walk around with the princesses all day." He popped a slice orange out of its peel tossing it into the air to catch into his mouth. Rory snatched it out of the air and ate the slice. With his mouth full of juice he said, "It was just another job. You know how it goes.". "No. I most certainly do not know how it goes.." He shot him an annoyed glance "… Hey do you think you can cover me tonight so that I can get out of here for a little while? I need a distraction." Lee asked wiping the juice off of his chin. "Lee, your whole life is one big distraction." Rory laughed. "No seriously. I will owe you one big Ri. I want to go see my mother. I miss her it's been just over 6 months now. You practically had the day off anyway.".

Rory sighed. He honestly didn't want to guard this ball tonight. He wanted to lay in his bed for once and relax, "Now you really owe me one." He finished with a half-hearted grin towards his friend. "Thank you!" He shouted grabbing his burlap sack and jumping up off of the crate they were sitting on. "Anything for you Lee." He said winking at his friend. "Watch yourself now Ri." He said with a laugh. "You're not my type." Rory said smugly. "I don't think you have a type my friend." He said with a laugh. Rory threw his shoe at the door. His friend looked at him with a fake appalled expression placing his hand on his chest.

A Violet Night

Laughing Rory watched as his friend walked away. He sighed and stood grabbing his shoe *"I guess I should get going too."* He thought to himself *"It's going to be one long night."*. He walked down to the bunks and changed into his 'proper' attire getting washed up as he went.

Rory took his shirt off and tossed it into the pile of dirty linen he needed to wash. "I thought I could find you here." Visha's shrill voice filled the air of his room as he turned around. *"Oh God."* He thought to himself. She approached him slowly draping her hands around his neck leaning into his neck to kiss it. "Not now." He said pushing her off calmly. "Don't be like that. I know what you want." She said in a low voice getting down on her knees for him. "Please, Visha not tonight I just don't feel up to this charade.". She looked up at him as she unbuckled his pants and put him in her mouth. He stared at the wall empty. He wasn't sure why *she* was running through his mind. He smiled at the thought of their conversation from earlier that day. "You like that?" Visha said as she continued harder. He looked down at her in disgust and sighed letting her continue placing his hand on the back of her head he grabbed a fistful of her hair.

She stood up wiping her mouth. "Lay with me?" She asked laying on his bed. "I can't. I need to get going. Lee conned me into his long shift so he can see his mom.". Visha started to laugh, he looked at her confused. "The only '*mommy*' Lee is going to see is the tits of the girls I do business with.". Rory looked at her unenthused. "I saw him before I left." She said taking her dress off and snuggling up under his blankets. "Of course he was there. If you sleep here again tonight try to be more conspicuous when you leave. My uncle has warned me to many times about having you down here in our chambers." He said looking at her in the mirror slipping his arms through his black sleeves. She smiled at him. "I snuck some more snacks from the kitchen. They are in the cupboard beside the bed with the extra candles." He said running his fingers through his hair. "Wake me up when you get back in." She said rolling over to face the wall.

He left and made his way up to the ball room. His uncle was down the hall "You don't look like Lee to me." He said placing both his hands on his belt buckle. "Well you know how it goes he gets diarrhea so bad one would think he has the plague". "Yeah, we will go with that son." He said with a small laugh "In that case. You will be in the North Hall. Sometimes these people 'wonder off'. It should be a quiet night over here for you.". "Thank you Uncle." Rory said. "Least I could do after the good job you did today watching over those two." He said patting him on his shoulder "So how was it today?". "It was... It was definitely something." Rory said with a nervous chuckle. "Yeah the niece is definitely something..." He said annoyed. "And the princess is definitely something else too." His uncle smacked his lips cutting to the chase "Oh, and you should tell Lee to expect more stable duties for now on.". "Can do." He said as his uncle started to walk away from him.

He leaned against the wall listening to the music and the laughter from the other side. He rubbed the sleep from his eyes and then ran his fingers through his hair. He knew he was in for a long night.

He looked over to the far entrance of the ball room. There she was. She was smiling at his uncle, who was no doubt telling her how beautiful she looked. And oh how she did look beautiful. He would give anything at this moment to get her out of his mind.

He looked away and stood straighter against the wall as a group of women walked past him. "This is useless. They will never find anyone for her. I mean just look at the poor darling.". "I heard there's only one man here who is actually interested in her and not for the throne.". "No. You don't mean? He's here?" another said fanning herself in awe "She could never deserve such a man like him.". The women nodded her head in agreeance.

"Good evening madams." Rory said redirecting them back towards the front entrance. He held the door for them as they continued to gossip. They didn't even notice his existence.

He looked inside. It was to vibrant, and alive. He looked up to the four large chairs centered at the head of the room at the grand table. He watched for her for a second. She looked lonely up there. Quickly he recomposed himself closing the door behind him. *I'm not going back in there.* He thought to himself. *"This has to stop now."*.

A Violet Night

<u>Chapter 6.)</u>

Violet stared at her reflection in the mirror. Her

hair was tucked away into a loose bun on top of her head,

her dress was tight fitting sage and lilac. "Look at you."

Harriet smiled admiring her work in the mirror. She stood

next to her in her pink sheer flowing dress. Her hair down

tucked neatly behind her ears with a pearl comb. "Oh

Violet I'm so happy for you. After all you're so lucky to

have this in your honor!" She shrieked "Who knows maybe

I will find someone tonight too.". She floated to the door

her head was in a different world. Violet stood up, her feet

felt like they were trapped inside of a pair of lead shoes.

"Violet! Let's go!" she said sternly coming out of her trance. She trudged her way behind her cousin. "Things will be alright love." Elda said putting her arm entangled in hers. She patted her hand smiling at her. Violet nodded at her with reassuring eyes.

Standing at the double doored back entrance to the ball room Violet paused and played with her silver laced mask in her hands turning it over and over nervously.

"Well don't you three look as ravishing as ever?" Her father's right-hand man said. He reached for Violets hand and spun her around. She smiled at him. Elda smacked his arm and laughed playfully. "Thank you." Violet said to him. "I wish you nothing but the best of luck tonight my dear." He said kissing her hand. She curtsied at him. "Not my girl. She does not require luck." Elda said with a smile at Violet. "No.. I suppose not when she learned from the best." He said smiling at Elda. Violet turned her head. Harriet had already gone inside without her. "Well go on now shoo." Elda said waving the palms of her hands at her.

She took a deep breath as she pushed through the doors that opened as easy as moving two large stones. She entered the room overlooking the back of her parents' heads. Into the cluster of men, and women wearing individually unique shaped made masks.

Violet took her place on her mother's left side. They sat at their table for what seemed like an eternity. Watching and greeting the guest while food was passed around their long table. "Go mingle." Her mother finally whispered just loud enough for her to hear. She finished off her glass and stood up. Walking herself through the crowd handing out small but subtle grins at passing strangers, grabbing hands with a few on her way around.

"Violet! Over here." She turned as she heard Harriet's voice just over the crowd. *"NO. Just NO."* she thought to herself as she began to walk towards her. A very drunken Harriet swaying slightly surrounding herself with 5 men. One set of red headed twins, one very tall dark-skinned man with a beard, an under averaged shorter man spilling his drink down his white shirt as he gulped his last few drops, and lastly the only one Harriet was paying any attention to, Niran.

Harriet has had feelings, very strong feelings at that for Niran ever since they were children.. He had the most copper golden locks for hair.

He grinned aggressively at Violet as his body shifted towards her presence "How nice of you to come down here with the rest of us for the evening.". He looked at her from head to toe and back up stopping to stare at her breast. Violet got an uneasy feeling in the pit of her stomach as she crossed her arms to cover herself. "It's nice to see you again Niran." She said out of politeness. "Yes. How very nice for you to join us." Harriet said sternly as she stood as a wedge between Niran and Violet. She took a step back "I can't spend all night up there after all." She said with an uneasy laugh. "No I suppose you can't." Niran said as he swirled around his glass in his hand looking back up at her "I'm going to get some more wine, do either one of you care for a refill?". Harriet quickly thrusts her glass into his hands, nodding her head up and down. He stared at Violet for a moment with his piercing brown eyes. She calmly shook her head and replied, "No thank you.". He shrugged his shoulders and walked off towards the barred table.

"Tonight's going to be the night." Harriet slurred as she put her hand on Violets shoulder for balance, "I can feel it in my bones. Look at the way he keeps looking over here at me. He was watching me at the table too!". Violet looked across the room at Niran. He was looking over at them, but she had that same uneasy feeling in her stomach as before when she made eye contact with him. She gently took Harriet's hand off her shoulder "I'm going to get some air.". Harriet looked at her as if she didn't understand what she was saying, but then quickly returned to gazing at Niran. She carefully glided her way back through the crowd and out one of the side exits.

Violet leaned against the closed door taking her mask off, and took a deep breath in. She began to walk down the long lightly light up hallway with not a soul in sight. Just her alone in her thoughts.

She pushed open a smaller stain glass door leading onto the stone balcony leaving it open behind her. She softly placed both hands on the railing of the balcony breathing in the calm nights air and overlooking the silence of the night on the treetops below. She let the mask drop from her fingers.

Violet watched the mask float gently to the ground. She felt two firm hands on her waist pulling her back onto someone's warm body. Pushing the hands off of her she spun around to come face to face with Niran. She could smell the strong aroma of alcohol on his breath. He stumbled a few steps behind himself.

Violets stomach suddenly felt sick again, as if it weighed 10 extra pounds. She took a step backwards until her back hit the railing. "Uhm, excuse you." She said disgusted. He grinned aggressively closing the door behind him and began to walk towards her with a fast pace. She continued to step to the right, and backwards until her back was now up against the wall. Her heart was now beating out of her chest as he shoved himself up against her. "Stop! Get off of me!" She screamed trying her hardest to shove him off of her. He pushed her hands over the top of her head holding them down swiftly with just one of his own hands.

Violet began to feel closed in. Her heart racing out of her chest. "Stop. Please stop! Please don't do this. Think about Ann!" She whispered through the tears forming in her eyes. He stopped kissing her neck and looked into her eyes "I saw the way you were looking at me Violet. I know you want me too. There is no reason to resist this any longer.".

She let out a whimper as the words spilled from his lips. She felt his other hand slowly slip down her dress as he began to pull it up farther. Violet began to sob harder trying to kick him off of her with all of her might "No. I wasn't looking at you honestly Niran I wasn't.". His cold hand touched her thigh giving her shivers. She closed her eyes and felt as if she could throw up. "Relax Violet." He said as if to comfort her, "If I cannot have Ann. Well.. then this is simply second best.". "Niran Please.." She whimpered. He looked up at her as if she was begging him to continue. He smiled devilishly at her. Violet cast her face to the side looking over the edge of the balcony as large heavy tears roamed her cheeks.

A Violet Night

<u>Chapter 7.)</u>

Rory yawned covering his mouth. He let his hand trace the wall as he walked exhaling. He glad this was his post for the night, and not guarding the inside of the ball. There are many less judging eyes in the hallways. Hell, there are no eyes in this hallway tonight.

The sound of a door down the hall startled him as he straightened himself up again. A woman shadow swiftly opened it and leaned heavily against it. Rory squinted his eyes down the hall to try to see what she was doing. There she was again. It was as if she was impossible to escape.

She began walking farther down the hall and split off onto a balcony.

The pace of his walk began to quicken, and he found himself standing in front of a small stain glass door. He paused smiling to himself. There she stood looking over the railing. "*Should I say something?*" he thought to himself "*Nah, why would she want to talk to me?*". His smile turned into a slight frown as he walked away.

He pushed her out of his mind as he walked farther from the door frame. "Be a sport and take this." He heard a man say looking up just in time to see a glass being tossed towards his face. He caught it with his right hand. "Oh. Good catch." The man said sarcastically grasping at the wall to hold himself up. Rory set the glass down on the small marble table next to him. Not saying a word he walked right passed him. "A man of few words I see? I like that." The man said as he too began to walk in the opposite direction of Rory. "The party is this way sir." He said to him. "Ah, so it is, but lucky for you I am going after my girl.".

Rory shook his head looking over his shoulder to see the man once again stumble and try to grasp the wall. A small laugh escaped his lips as he watched.

Once he reached the end of the assigned hallway Rory thought to himself about the snarky conversations he had with the princess earlier that day and made himself a small promise that if she was still there when he walked passed a second time that he would talk to her. He had too. Maybe this is what it would take to get her out of his mind if he could only talk to her one more time.

The door was closed this time around. He bit the inside of his lip listening to the distressed muffled voiced on the other side of the door. *"This is not your business."* He told himself as he turned to continue walking. He took two steps before turning right back around and opening the door. He saw the drunken man shoved up against the princess. "No. I wasn't looking at you honestly Niran I wasn't." He heard her say through her tears.

Without thinking he shoved the man off of her not hearing the words he had responded to her. The man bounced off of the wall looking surprised and pissed he readjusted his clothes. "Alright mate, I think you should be going now." He said angrily taking a step back towards her. Rory stepped in front of her "You need to leave." He said sternly. He felt her breath on his back. The man opened his mouth to speak but Rory cut him off grabbing his shirt and shoving him out of the door. Staggering his way back into the door frame he said "So we just go after men who are in-incom-" Rory cut him off "Incapacitated. Yes." He said nodding his head giving him a final shove out he doorway. He waited and watched as he stumbled off cussing in a rage down the hallways.

A Violet Night

He turned around. The princess was now sitting on the small bench drying her tears with both hands. "Are you okay?" He asked. She nodded her head "I'm better now that you're here." She said with an uneasy laugh. He didn't know what to do. Was he supposed to keep his distance or comfort her?

There was a long silence, "Well then I should be getting back to my post." He said uneasily turning back to the door. "No! Please stay." Violet said startled as she scooted over on the bench making room for him. *"Don't sit down."* He thought to himself as he sat down next to her.

"I can't stay long. There's no one on my hall.". "Don't do that." She said as if she was offended "Don't do what?" He asked. "Don't act like this isn't better then walking up and down these halls all night long looking for stragglers and making sure no one urinates in the potted trees." She said with a small laugh. Rory let out a small grin. She was right he would rather be here then back out in the hall. "Do you want to talk about what just happened?" Rory asked in a confused tone. Violet shook her head aggressively "Nope, not in the slightest bit.".

"So tell me about this '*Dangerous*' little village we apparently have." Violet said breaking the silence. "You don't really want to hear about that." He said not breaking his concentration on the stars above. She shoved his arm "Yes, I really do. No one's ever said anything about it to me until you did. I didn't even know it existed until today." She laughed a little. "You took off in that direction, so you have to know a little about it." He said to her tightening his grip on the bench. She could no longer read his expression "I just took off in whatever direction Lola wanted to go in.".

He looked at her as she laughed and smiled. For a split second he forgot who they were. As if they weren't from two entirely different social classes in life. His smile soon faded "What? It's not like you grew up in there."

Violet said with a grin. His silence was obvious to her.

Rory scooted himself away from her on the bench "But I did." He said quietly.

A Violet Night

Chapter 8.)

She felt so stupid, but how was she supposed to know. "I'm so-". "What? You're sorry? Don't be. Not everyone can be born into luxury like you." He cut her off "It's not like you honestly want to hear about it anyway." He stood up walking towards the door. "Rory wait. I didn't know." She said turning around on the bench. "No. How could you." He murmured with a hint of sarcasm turning back around to face her.

"I don't remember telling you my name." He said softly changing the subject. Violet felt slightly embarrassed again as she felt her cheeks start to blush "Well, it was pretty rude of you to not tell me your name after you ran me down." She said sternly with a grin. "So you were asking about me?" He asked flashing his teeth.

With a blank expression he walked up to her taking her hand in his. He shook her hand "My name is Rory Guerrero.". She laughed as she shook his hand back with a squeeze "I am Violet, Violet Azazel Seathers.". "Oh, so we are getting formal telling me your middle name now?" He said with a devilish grin. "Well.. Now you know my complete name, you know, in case you need to ever fully address me." She said letting go of his hand. He laughed "Yeah okay. I think if any of my superiors ever were to overhear me say anything other than 'My Lady' or 'Your' Highness' they'd slap the shit out of me.". "When you are with me I want you to call me Violet. In fact I order you to call me Violet. It makes me feel like I'm not up on some high pedicle." she said watching him walk over to the railing and putting his backside to it facing her. He crossed his arms and feet studying her curiously ..

A Violet Night

She looked down at her hands shyly while she played with her dress. She frowned as the flashbacks of the evening set in. She wanted to change her clothes. She just felt so dirty as if no bath in her lifetime could ever make her feel clean again.

"Paolo." He said breaking the silence. "What?" She asked looking back up at him. "That's my middle name. It only seems fair to let you know mine since you suddenly felt obligated to tell me yours. You know in case you ever want to 'fully' address me.". She smiled watching his eyes overpower her.

"I am sorry though. I really didn't know you grew up that way." She said sincerely. Rory paused taking a moment to think of how to approach her as he walked over to the bench hesitantly sitting back down next to her with sadness in his voice "It is not what you think.. I was nine when my mother passed away.". "I'm sorry… May I ask what happened to her?" Violet asked feeling as if she was intruding. He stared hesitantly at Violet before continuing "You will need to stop apologizing. My life is not some tragedy for your entertainment Princess. If in the case you are insinuating in any way, no. My mother was not some harlot. No, she was very kind and soft spoken. She would have done anything for someone in need. Even if it meant giving you all she had... she would go hungry before she watched a stranger starve." He scoffed to himself with a lighthearted smile. It faded instantly as his eyes became hard "Now my father on the other hand. He- he was a drunken man. I don't think there was a day that went by where he did not drown himself in spirits or was hitting on my mother... She used to try to hide the bruises you know? when I was little that is." He paused letting his mind drift pondering if he should continue.

Violet shifted her body posture farther in his direction until their knees touched. It had caught him off guard. She could tell as his body stiffened, but he left their knees touching. She folded her hands inside her lap.

"One day we were carrying back goods from town. When she stopped me in the middle of the roadway. There were 3 men in the road standing over a body on the ground, and they were just laughing at the corpse. One kicking it as he did so. She told me quietly to hide in the bushes next to us. Being a child of course, I did what I was told not realizing how loud I was being as I did so.".

Violet inched closer to him as he continued to speak still looking away from her. "What happened?" She asked softly. "They took turns with her, and when they finished they slit her throat.. All I could do was watch from the bushes, frozen to afraid to even open my mouth.

Then when they were done and gone after all of our goods where picked through I covered her with her torn clothing, and I laid with her. All night I laid in the dirt with her. Wishing I could die right there with her. Word must have gotten to my uncle that night about what had happened because in the morning I awoke to him picking me up. He tried his best to shield me from looking at my mother's covered but lifeless body hanging off his horse.. I still remember the color of the blood mixed with the dirt and how it stained the ground in the early morning hours. The cold dew on the grass, and musty air that pierced my nostrils. He brought me back here. Fed me, clothed me, took care of me, and taught me everything I now know. We, we uh- buried her some place no one would ever find her except the two of us. A place where her and my uncle grew up." .

Rory stopped himself. He had never told anyone that before. He looked over to his side, Violet was looking up at him with no outward emotion. He felt a flutter in the pit of his stomach as he looked into her eyes. They dilated as she looked back into his own. Something that made him feel comfortable. Rory stood up abruptly *"No. I'm not doing this."* He thought to himself.

Violet looked up at him still being silent. "My parents hate me for not being my dead sister, and for looking like my dead brother. I know because I see it in their eyes every time they look or even talk to me. I isolate myself to avoid the disappointment in their faces and the sly comments they make. The only person who has ever shown me true kindness in this lifetime is Elda. She is more my mother then my own has ever been to me." She said coming now face to face with him. Violet was so close to him that he could feel her labored breathing on him. "I know that is nowhere close to what you've been through, but you can trust me. This world is far too large for us to have no one.".

Rory coughed clearing his throat moving away from her. His heart was racing. He could feel his hands shaking "Do you want me to walk you back to your room? I don't think he's still out there, but you never know.". She silently nodded her head at him biting the inside of her lip nervously.

He opened the door for her peeking his head out in both direction before telling her it was safe to go. She hugged him taking the breath out of his chest. Catching him off guard he did not know what to do. After a few seconds he hugged her back with on hand behind her back and the other behind her head pulling her to his chest. "Thank you." She whispered with a tremble on her tongue. "You're welcome.. Violet.". She smiled up at him genuinely.

He tried to avoid looking down into her eyes and cleared his throat letting go of her he once again opened the door to let her out. He could see her still smiling out of the corner of his eye. She shoved him in the chest playfully as she exited. He followed her out close behind. She grabbed onto his arm right arm. He looked around frantically. "Oh relax! We are the only two people in this entire kingdom not inside the ballroom walls." She said trying to calm his

nerves "Besides, if anyone asks you can simply tell them

I've had far too much to drink tonight, and I needed

someone to lean on.". "And that is the one I will use if we

see anyone." He said with a laugh still trying to give

himself from her body.

A Violet Night

Chapter 9.)

They laughed and talked all the way to her room.
"Well, this is it." She said still giggling from his bad jokes.
Violet put both of her hands behind her back and leaned
against the door. Awkwardly miscalculating the distance
behind her and hitting the door with a thud.

"Yeah, I guess I'll see you around then." He said
nervously running his fingers through his hair. They stared
at each other and then with a smile "Okay, goodnight
then.". He smiled reaching in past her, coming so close to
her that he could smell the lavender on her skin. He pushed
open her bedroom door. Pulling his body back he grinned

at her nodding his head and turning around "Sweet

dreams…Violet.". He liked the way her name felt in his

mouth. He glanced over his shoulder as she closed the door

slowly.

Rory didn't understand. He had been around many

women and yet not one of them has made him feel this way

to this extent like she does. Everything in his body was

telling him to turn around. *"No. This is wrong."* He thought

to himself *"Just keep walking. You do not want these*

problems…. Fuck it…".

The flutters in his stomach grew larger as he turned

back around. He wanted to be sick. Raising his hand to

knock on the door as it came open "Yes?" Violet asked.

Rory took a deep breath in as he grabbed her face with his

two hands and kissed her slowly. He knew this was wrong,

but he didn't care. She grabbed his wrist and pulled herself

up onto her tiptoes kissing him back softly. "Goodnight

Violet." Rory whispered into her ear as he let her face go

gently. Violet looked up at him smiling wildly. Her eyes wide with excitement and whispered back "Goodnight Rory.".

Violet closed the door, and slowly slid her back down it until her bottom hit the floor. *"What just happened?"* she questioned to herself. Her belly was full of butterflies and her heart was still racing to the thought of his voice and his breath still hot in her ear. "This is wrong." She said out loud biting her knuckle as she stood up getting undressed for bed. She blew out the candles and crawled into bed underneath the thin covers.

The next morning Violet found herself floating down to breakfast. She just kept replaying the night before in her head over and over. She smiled to herself as her hand ran along the cold stone wall guiding her fingers through the rough gravel grooving. She could feel every dimple, every crevice through her fingertips.

A Violet Night

"Was it that good of a night?" Elda asked not looking up from the bowl she was mixing on the countertop. "Hmm, oh uh. Yeah I suppose it was alright." Violet said placing both of her hands on the countertop next to her. Elda smacked the bowl down next to her hands "You met someone, didn't you?". Violet shook her head looking down "No ma'am.". "Honey, I know you better than that." She said gently using her index finger to push Violets chin up. She smiled at Elda and opened her mouth to speak but was cut off by a familiar sounding voice from behind them.

"Good morning Elda!" Rory said joyfully as he strolled in from behind them. He skittishly paused as he cleared his throat and made eye contact with Violet "Good morning my lady.". She nervously smiled back at him. She could feel her heart start to race again as he spoke in her direction. She looked back down at the floor then back at him "Yes, it is a good morning.".

A Violet Night

He smiled at her again this time showing more of his teeth as he grabbed a cookie from the jar on the counter reaching past her so close that they nearly touched with their clothes. Violet held her breath "Well, I have to get going now. Ladies. May you both have a golden day.". He looked back and forth from Elda winking at Violet. She watched him drift into the garden from the door frame.

Elda looked at the door then back at Violet. She took the spoon out of the bowl and popped Violets hand with it just enough to make it sting. "Him?!" She exclaimed. Her scolded brow turned into a loud laugh "Ooh child, I don't think you know what you're doing.". Violet rubbed her hand. That was the truth. Violet had no idea what she was doing with him. All she knew was that she felt safe when he was around. She felt safe, and for once she actually felt happy.

"Well do go on my dear. Spill the beans." Elda said returning to her stirring. Violet told Elda everything that had happened last night with Niran and with Rory.

Elda looked at Violet with concern "Although I am incredibly grateful to see my girl happy. You need to make sure this is what you want before you go any farther with him Violet. This could potentially be dangerous for the both of you. More so him then you.". Violet nodded her head "I know,". "I do not think that you do quite yet my dear.." Elda whispered putting her hand on top of hers and patting it gently "Now, go on. You know you're not supposed to be down here with me as much as I love your company.".

Nodding her head again Violet started walking towards the garden door. Elda shook her head back and forth nervously laughing "Mmmmmm. This is going to be trouble.". Elda took a drink out of the glass on the countertop. Walking to the window she gently pushed it open careful not to make a sound. Staying out of sight she watched as Violet looked around the garden. "Do we have anymore oats?" one of the servers asked. Elda quickly shut the window standing in front of it. "In the pot." She said pointing to the pot over a dull flame. "Another bird got in or you just needed some air? Because you never have that open unless you're cooling something baked." She asked looking at Elda with suspicion.

"Yes, a noisy bird just flew in asking about some oats." She said pouring some into a bowl and shoving it into her hands. The girl looked at her with her eyes big. "Don't ask me my business again child." She said with a smile "I don't ask you how to serve the food. Don't ask me about my kitchen.". "Yes ma'am.." she said with a stutter. "Out you go." She said pointing to the door. Elda looked back at the window "Trouble indeed..".

A Violet Night

Chapter 10.

Violet led herself into the garden, she looked around aimlessly. She turned in every which direction disappointed that she did not see Rory. "Are you following me?" She heard Rory say as he came from around one of the big leafy trees. "Trying too, but I don't seem to be doing such a great job at it." she said walking towards his deep graveled voice.

He looked around and grabbed her by the wrist lightly "Come on now beautiful. We mustn't be seen together like this.. Out here it's too risky.". He began to walk ahead of her. She happily followed without hesitation.

A Violet Night

Outside of the garden walls Rory looked around at the hilled empty field and the tree line that blanketed the surrounding area before he pushed Violet against the round tan and red stones with one hand on the arch of her back and the other on the wall just above her head. He watched her eyes dilate with excitement before kissing her. She smiled up at him again he stared at her taking the moment in. He took a deep breath in and fixed her hair behind her ear.

"Ahemm." A voice said from behind Rory. "Shit. Stay behind me." He whispered, keeping Violet hidden behind him. He slowly turned around. Lee looked at him and then trying to look around him curiously he said "I just uhh, wanted to thank you again for covering my post last night.". "You are more than welcome." He responded as he blocked Violet with his arm from moving forward. "Is that her?" He mouthed at Rory, still curiously trying to look around him. "Who?" He mouthed back at him. Lee stood there giving Rory a *"Are you kidding me look."*.

Standing up straight he acted as if he was fixing his crown, then began to royally wave at him. Letting out a snicker Rory sighed and stepped out of the way. He knew how huge of a risk he was taking by doing this, but Lee is like a brother to him. If he could trust anyone in this place it would be him.

"OH SHIT!" Lee shouted leaning forward intrigued covering his mouth with his fist "I'm sorry your highness, I didn't mean to shout it's just- wow.". Violet was confused, and a little bit frightened. How could he just expose them like this? Rory looked at her reassuringly then back at Lee "Oh no," Lee laughed "Trust me your highness. Your secret is safe with me. Seriously, we all have our skeletons in our closets locked away somewhere. Maybe not one this big that could have two of us gruesomely executed but.. none the less we all have our skeletons.". He came closer to the pair and put his hand forward. Violet cautiously shook his hand as he bowed before her. "Don't do that." She said as he looked at her confused. "She wants to be treated like one of us." Rory said sarcastically tucking his thumbs in his waistband.

Laughing again Lee said "One of us? Oohh, no that's not what you want.". "Don't you have somewhere to be Lee?" Rory asked pulling Lee away from Violet by his elbow who was still holding onto her hand. "You know what? I actually do have somewhere to be. You are lucky this time Ri." He looked back at Violet, "It was a pleasure to finally meet you.". "Same to you." She replied with a wave. Rory took a few steps with Lee forward "You need to be more careful man. I could have been anyone." Lee said concerned "You know I think this is crazy right? They could put your head on the wall for this. Accuse you of some crazy shit. Or worse they could put me up there with you for conspiracy."

A Violet Night

"Don't you think I know that?" Rory said quietly, although to tell the truth he had not put much thought into his actions at all. He had been so caught up in the moment with her. The reality of the situation began to sink in. It scared him. Lee nodded and smacked him on the back, waving again at Violet he took off walking into the garden shaking his head still in disbelief.

"So.. That just happened.. Who was he again?" Violet asked trying her best to remain calm. "Yeah, yeah it sure did… That would be Lee, he's more or less my brother." He said walking back to her. "Are you alright?" She asked. He shook his head yes and snatched her hand up "Come on lets go somewhere more secret.".

"Where are you supposed to be today?" she asked with concern in her tone. "Anywhere and everywhere princess." He said with a grin "But most importantly I am supposed to be with you.". A shiver of excitement went through her spine. He led her to a small shed outside the garden. It smelled of rotting wood and earth tools, but he closed the door behind him. It was hot and dark. The damp moisture filled the air with little slits of sunshine shining through onto their bodies. She hyper fixated on the way the sun rays hit his eyes. "You're so beautiful." He said to her with a genuine smile. "Easy for you to say it's nearly pitch black in here." She laughed. "Even a blind fool could see how beautiful you truly are Violet.".

She laughed nervously trying to dodge his compliment "So this is the plan for the day?". "No.. but this is." He said pulling her face close to hers with his hands.

A Violet Night

Chapter 11.)

Three months of secret meetings came and went. Each one better than the last. The rush of excitement filled them with every secret encounter. Harriet had returned back to her own kingdom after extending her stay twice to entertain the idea of her and Niran. The castle had been overly calm ever since.

"Violet," Rory paused. She looked up from his lap as he continued to play with her long hair "Do you think this is a mistake?". She looked at him confused "Do you ever think what we are doing is a mistake Ri?" before he could answer she sat up "Because I honestly don't care if this is one. You make me happy and for once that is but enough for me.". He smiled at her and kissed her forehead to calm her down "You make me happy too." He whispered. "Good." She said as she pushed him in the chest and took off running. He pretended to let her blow knock him over clutching his chest as he toppled over dramatically.

He shook his head "*She's wild.*" He thought to himself. He let her get a head start into the trees before he took off after her in a full sprint.

Rory put his hands behind his back catching his breath. He said playfully "I guess I lost her.". He shrugged his shoulders, "I guess I'm free from my master at last. I could run away to the ocean and feel the sea salt on my face every morning and the sand under my toes.".

He heard laughter from his right. Violet was sitting on a lower branch of a tree. "There go all my plans." He said with a disappointed laugh as he walked over to her evenly distributing both of his hands on the branch that she was sitting on. Rory climbed up on the branch and sat with her in silence. simply enjoying one another's company with her head on his shoulder. This was his favorite place to be.

Once the sound of the pond frogs and cicadas filled their ears he knew it was time to venture back to the castle. Rory hopped off of the branch and motioned Violet on to follow him.

"Can't we just stay here?" She said blissfully leaning back. "Before morning rise they would have an entire search party out for you, and my head on a spike in town square for everyone to view the kidnapper of the princess." Rory said admiring her. She jokingly agreed nodding her head "Yeah although I wonder what color spike they would put you on?". "Probably silver I suppose." He laughed at her morbid joke "Will you make sure it's a blue one? I'm pretty fond of that color now days.". "Done deal." She said kissing his cheek.

Holding hands they made their way to the garden entrance. "I'll come find you tomorrow sometime." He said kissing her forehead. She smiled and stretched on her tip toes to kiss his lips. Their hands fell to their sides as they walked in opposite directions to their opposite lives.

"What the actual hell is going on around here?" Harriet said as Violet walked into the kitchen. "Hmm?" Violet said surprised to see her. Harriet's demeanor changed suddenly from anger to calmness in her face and her posture relaxed "You know I should tell your father about what you and that raggedy guard have been doing together.".

Violet opened her mouth to either defend herself or cry she was not sure. "Relax cousin. I am not going to say anything about your *little* rendezvous with rag boy... It is nice to not see you mopping around for once. I suppose we all need our own little distractions.". Violet went in for a hug. She never imagined herself ever doing so to Harriet. "Hmph. No ma'am." Harriet said connecting her palms with Violets' shoulder stiffly.

"I have something to tell you!" Harriet exclaimed. She looked at her cousin intrigued. "I spent the night with Niran, and oh Violet it was wonderful! He came to our castle to discuss business with my father and snuck into my chamber when they were finished. It was simply magical. I understand now why Ann was so infatuated with him.". Violet was more than a little disgusted at Harriet's news, but she did her best to not let it show in her face.

"Why are you really here, because I know you didn't travel all this way to tell me about your sex life Harriet." Violet said forcing a smile on her lips. Harriet sighed and took Violets hand looking around the empty room pulling her out of the kitchen and into the pantry closet.

"Why are we in the closet?" Violet asked confused. "Our fathers are about to go to war with the Eastern Kingdom... They have attacked my fathers' outpost in between our fathers kingdoms. My father has moved me here for protection for the remainder of the war." Harriet said full of worry looking through the slots on the pantry door. Violet looked at her shocked "What? The Eastern Kingdom?". Harriet nervously bit her lip nodding her head "He says it is far better guarded here against the enemies of the outside. Wait? You didn't know about this?". "No! I most definitely was not informed." Violet's voice took to concern. "I suppose this is supposed to be hushed business then... I heard them say this morning they are going to start to round up the guards and knights tonight from both kingdoms and send the first line up into battle.".

"No." She said upset. She had finally found someone she could be herself around, and now potentially she could lose him too? "I have to warn him." Violet whispered. "Warn him? From what Violet? Are you going to warn him about his own duty to your father? His duty to the kingdom, to you even? You can't protect him if he is chosen, and he hides they will kill him for treason. If he is picked, and he goes all we can do is hope for the best." Harriet said grasping her wrist tight. Violet looked at her teary eyed "It will be alright." Harriet whispered embracing her cousin for the first time genuinely. She could honestly feel the empathy in her cousins voice.

Violet's heart and head were bombarded with a sudden whirlwind of emotions as she silently pulled back. She knew she would have to do something, anything. She could not lose him. Not now. Harriet opened the pantry door. "Were you looking for something in particular?" a maid asked. As Harriet spoke to the woman Violet flooded out past her with no idea of where to go, or what to do.

She sped walked down to the guards chambers. She spotted Lee in the hallway "Have you seen Rory?" she asked trying to remain calm. He shook his head at her taking her by the shoulders and pulling her immediately out of sight "You can check his room, but I don't think he is down here. Honestly neither should you be.". She looked at him harshly. He sighed and let go of her shoulders. He pointed down the clay and stone hallway "Second to last room on the right.". She nodded to him and walked hastily to open the door. It was empty not even a candle lit. She looked around his unkept room inhaling sharply. She closed the door and sat down on his bed. She nervously sat up and began to fold his clothes that were thrown about.

She picked up the last of his shirts and smelled it. Her stomach felt sick as she began to think about the situation at hand. She rushed to tidy up the rest of the space making his bed and putting things away neatly.

A knock at the door startled her as she hid behind the opening door. Holding her breath as someone peeked in. Lee stepped inside "Princess you need to get out of here. They are doing nightly room checks to make sure no one is down here that isn't supposed to be.". He grabbed her by the lower arm.

The sudden sound of footsteps outside the doorway made their stomachs drop. Their eyes widened at each other. "Get under the bed." He said to her shoving her down lightly. The door began to open as Lee shoved himself against it. "Gomez?" a familiar voice said. Violet scooted herself as far as she could until she felt the wall against her back. She watched the boots scuffle around the room. She held her breath hoping no one would hear her. "Lose another bet did ya?" the captain said opening the closet door and reshutting it promptly. "Yes sir. Sure did."

Lee said nervously standing in front of the bed. "I'll trust you're the only one in here then. I have to get to a meeting. Tell my nephew to try and keep it clean this time... Oh, and Gomez next time, don't forget to dust." He said taking a minute to scrape his finger across the shelving by the door and leaving the room.

Once the door closed and a few moments passed, Lee helped Violet out from underneath the bed. "I'm sorry I didn't mean to shove you like that." He said. "It's alright." She said readjusting herself "Where is he?". "Sometimes he disappears like this, goes somewhere peaceful to think.". "When you see Rory will you let him know it's important?". "Is everything alright?" He asked.

"We are at war Lee." She whispered, "And I'm worried-.". "He might be picked for the first line up." He finished for her. Putting his feelings aside he said, "Come on... Let me help you back to your room.". He cupped her hands in comfort "That, a minute ago? That was far too much stress to handle.". She let out a smile. "No," he said

opening the door looking both ways two times over "You

think I am joking? I am not sure how you two enjoy this

much excitement I mean honestly. Rory almost came back

to a big ol' surprise on his rug.".

A Violet Night

Chapter 12.)

Violet wiped her face with some water in front of her mirror. She paused, watching the water droplets roll off her face. "What am I doing?" She asked herself angrily. "I cannot just sit around and let these things happen.".

Suddenly, She felt compelled to run up to her father's meeting quarters. She knocked repeatedly. "Come in." She heard her father heavy voice say. Violet could not contain herself as she burst open the door to a room full of superiors and commanders. All staring at her as she rushed in at her fathers' side. She knew she was not supposed to be

in the room with them for this type of meeting, but she
didn't care.

Her father looked up and stopped writing from his
scrolls. The white feather in his deep tan hand illuminated
in Violets eyes; it terrified her that he could have already
written Rory's name on that script as he folded his hands
on top of the thin paper.

"Father, I have learned the news of the incoming
war.". "And why do you wish to interrupt me daughter?".
"As I said, I have learned of the upcoming war with the
Eastern kingdom.. And I have come to ask if I could have
extra protection with me at all times. A guard that could
stay with me throughout the majority of the day and one for
Harriet as well.". One of the commanders let out a snicker.
"Silence! Is my daughters fear amusing to you?" The king
said raising his hand looking at the older man with the long
white beard. "No sir." He said looking back down at the
table embarrassed.

A Violet Night

Her father exhaled loudly "If that is what would make you feel the safest my daughter, then the guards' will take shifts with you around the clock.". She made eye contact with the Captain. He could see the fear in her eyes. Violet opened her mouth to speak. "Your Majesty if I may? Shifts would be terribly risky, you never know who could be playing both fields. I know two of your finest that would take nothing but the upmost pride best care of your daughter and your niece sir. Gomez, and Guerrero." He said turning all of his attention to the king.

He took his glasses off of his face studying his daughters posture "Then I suppose they can guard Harriet and yourself during the time of the war.". Violet curtsied "Oh, thank you father!" She said grateful looking back and forth between them both. "Now go. Let me return to my business." He said shooing her out of the room with his thunderous voice.

A Violet Night

Violet closed the quarters doors behind her. She had to go tell Rory the good news. She found herself sneaking back down to the guards' chambers. Racing in and out of the shadows to Rory's room. Knocking on the door she could not help but feel pure excitement to tell him. Rory opened the door in confusion wearing only a pair of pants and a tired look on his face. When he realized that it was indeed Violet standing at his door and not a walking dream he rushed her inside. "Are you mad?! You could have been spotted!" He choked out sleepily. Violet proceeded to tell him everything that had just unfolded in the hours past.

"You would do that for me?" He asked astonished. "Well it wasn't just me your uncle also had a say in it.". "You would do that for me? A nobody, who quite honestly deservers to go to war and die in battle.". "Why would you say that?" She asked sounding appalled "Rory, you are the most kind and lighthearted soul I have ever met. You talk to low about yourself as if you're not worthy of someone else's care or someone else's love.". He looked at her in the most loving way possible. Almost boy like "I love you Violet.". She kissed him "I love you more Rory.". "Most." He whispered kissing her again slower letting his tongue seep into her mouth. "Forever." She said climbing on top of him pushing him farther back onto his small bed.

He gripped her waist in both of his hands "Always" he whispered tightening his grip. She wrapped her arms around his neck. His hands slid down her backside. He squeezed it in his hands. Her heart began to race even harder. "Are you sure you are ready for this?" He asked kissing her neck. She nodded her head. She began to breath heavier as he undid her dress lace by lace slowly exposing her breast. She was ready for him. He kissed her body up and down. His hands traced all of her curves. He flipped her onto her back in one motion, kissing her still and pulling his pants down as she scrambled to get out of the rest of her dress tossing it to the side of the bed.

A Violet Night

He climbed back on top of her rubbing himself against her. She let out a moan. "We can stop." He whispered to her. She shook her head aggressively "No. Please don't." She begged squirming underneath him. He brought his chest to hers as he entered her. They both gasped in pleasure. She grabbed his hair and his back pulling him deeper inside. "Fuck." He whispered in her ear.

He pulled her on top of him as he leaned against the wall. He watched her bounce up and down as he held her hips. Moving one hand to her cheek she leaned her face against it slowing down. "I wish I could stay in this moment forever." He said looking father then her eyes. She leaned in and kissed him "Me too my love." She whispered against his lips.

A Violet Night

Chapter 13.)

"I wish I could stay right here with you." Violet
said curling up on his chest while their bare bodies clung to
one another. "I wish you could to." He said holding her
hand tight giving it a kiss before placing it on top of his
sternum. She watched in existential bliss as his chest rose
and fell. Full on comfort she closed her eyes listening to his
soft breathing.

Without any warning the door burst open. A women
stormed inside. Violet threw her head underneath the
covers in hopes that she did not see her face. "So this is
why you haven't given me the light of day huh Ri? Fucking

around with another I see?" She shouted angrily. Rory sat

on the side of the bed letting the blanket drape his lower

half.

"Visha, I told you already. We are finished. There

was never an us to begin with, nor will there ever be an

us.". "Right, so you did not mean any of those things you

said to me ever? All those long nights I just meant nothing

to you? So that you could just ignore me for weeks on end.

Avoiding me in the halls and keeping your door locked at

night. All this and for what? Just so you could screw a

someone new?" With saying that Visha ripped the blanket

off the bed exposing a naked Violet and Rory. Visha

dropped the blanket on the ground and cupped her mouth

with both of her hands. Violet scrambled to cover herself.

"Visha, please leave this in this room. No one needs to get

hurt from this okay? We had a miscommunication, and I

should have told you upfront that your services were no

longer required." Rory said calmly giving Violet the

blanket back to cover up with. He slid his pants back on

now standing halfway in between the two of them. Violet

looked around horrified and confused at the conversation.

"I don't know what to say. I'm sorry your

highness." Visha whispered taking a step farther towards

the door. Violet was still in too much of a shock to answer

her. Visha looked at Rory her face full of hurt and scurried

out of the room. "You should go." Rory said worried

handing Violet her dress without looking at her. She

quickly put it back on rushing out of the room.

Violet wanted to be sick, her stomach and chest hurt

so badly. She reached for a column in the hallway resting

her hands on it to regain herself. The sound of faint crying

fell upon her ears from the bench up the way from her.

Violet paused for a minute not knowing whether to

stop or continue walking past. "Are you okay?" She

whispered to her coming closer. "It's my own fault for

getting involved with a client like that, so just do us both a favor. Cut the act and leave me alone." Visha said cutting her a look and wiping away her tears, "He is nothing special anyways, as you will soon find out. Now if you will excuse me your highness I have a client waiting on me. One who will actually pay for my services. A very wealthy well known one indeed.". She said sucking up her tears with a sniffle. She looked at Violet as her eyes hardened and pushed past her.

Violet continued to her room terrified of what just occurred. She was awestruck at how a magical night could turn into such a disaster in such a short amount of time.

Laying in her bed Violet wiped a tear from her eye. She didn't exactly know if she was crying over the situation or if she genuinely pitied the women. Either way Violet was not going to be able to sleep that night. She felt as if she could throw up.

A Violet Night

How could they have been caught on three separate occasions? The first time they had gotten away with, the second time she had just simply gotten lucky, but now the third time? With a complete stranger at that. Well, a stranger to Violet anyways. She clearly knew Rory. She got up and walked around the room nervously biting her nails.

She sat on her balcony leaning against the wall all night until the sun arose on her cheeks, and the birds began singing in her ears. "What am I going to do?" She said to herself out loud. Elda sat next to her on the floor quietly.

"Is this seat taken?" She asked. Violet shook her head as her eyes became swollen with tears "That was very brave thing of you to do Violet." She said, "Talking to your father like that.". "I know it was risky." She said awaiting her disappointment "Risky? Yes, very risky. But love is full of risk my dear, and if this is what you want… If *he* is what you want. This is only the beginning of a long fight you will have to face for it.". Violet looked at her, her lip quivered "What if I'm not strong enough to fight this fight?" She asked. "My child, he is not the only fighter here. Look at everything you too have overcome in your short life. You cannot reap the benefits if you do not plant the seeds." Elda kissed her on the cheek "Come on now help me up I am far too old to be down on this ground with you.".

Violet let out a smile and pulled her to her feet. "Come now." She said pulling back the covers on her bed. Violet slipped in while Elda covered her patting her hair softly. "I will tell everyone to give you space today. That you are not feeling well. Monthly women troubles.".

"Thank you.." She whispered with her eyes already heavy. Elda leaned down giving her forehead a kiss.

A Violet Night

Chapter 14.)

"Wow." Lee said going through the basket on Rory's table trying to find a piece food that wasn't rock hard. "I just can't believe you didn't lock the door!" Lee said letting out a laugh. "It was the heat of the moment. I wasn't thinking." Rory said pouring some whiskey into a glass and sitting next to Lee at the table.

Lee shrugged his shoulders "I mean it is your own fault really. You will just have to hope she keeps her trap shut out of fear. I mean that or you could kill her?". Rory choked on the whiskey and laughed putting his glass down on the table. As good as that sounded to him he knew he could never do that to her. He never fully loved her, but he did care about her just enough to not want to see her dead or harmed in anyway.

Lee spent the rest of the evening trying to keep Rory's mind off of the situation. "Just get some rest Ri. Everything will be fine." Lee said opening the door to leave. *"Easy for you to say."* Rory thought to himself. He waved at his friend shutting the door.

"Fuck." He said out loud falling backwards on the bed. Rory ran his fingers through his hair multiple times each time more aggressive then the last. "Fuck!" He shouted again as he turned and punched his pillow. He laid back down on his back. He knew this anger would not help him, although it did feel good to get it out. He let out a loud sigh as he rolled over on his side where Violet had laid. It was still impossible in his mind that she had laid herself in his bed. He could still smell her on his sheets. He traced the pillow where her head had laid covering it with her thick dark hair.

Rory's mind was in a whirlwind. Why would she stick her neck out for him not to go to war? He could not wrap his mind around that thought. He let out a simple smile. For how could her of all women like someone of his stature? Someone so low on the chain of command.

Maybe that is why she liked him he thought to himself. That maybe just maybe she wanted someone lower than her in power to feel like a 'normal' person. Even if that was true, and what they have now is short lived. At least he felt whole, he felt needed, and most of all he felt heard.

He finally found himself dozing off and awoke to the sun streaming into his eyes. He cradled his head with his left hand. His head was pounding. He rubbed his eyes as he sat on the side of the bed. All the while he had been asleep he had not dreamt of what had happened last night. He wished he could go back to that. Washing his face in the bowl on his counter the images of last night replayed in his mind. He wished he'd of just locked the door the second he ushered her inside. Maybe he shouldn't have opened it to begin with.

Taking another shot while readying himself for the day he left for his post. Correction, he left for his *new* post, guarding of the princess. He still could not fathom that just a short while ago he was simply minding the stable with Lee, and now they were here. Life is crazy in that sense. When it moves it surely moves quick and in the blink of an eye at that.

He stopped at Lee's room knocking once before opening it "I know man I know. I'm coming he said tiding up his bed.". "I thought we could go past the kitchen before reporting to our new post." Lee closed his door.

"Boys." His uncle said to them heading down the hall "I'm sure you are aware of the changes made?". *"God please play dumb Lee."* He thought to himself "Changes?" Lee asked. "Yes. It seems you two chumps have lucked out. You will now be guarding the royal heirs." He looked at Rory worried.

Rory broke eye contact looking over at the wall "Thank you." they both said graciously. "I don't think it is me you should be thanking... Can I talk to you?" he said looking at his nephew. Lee leaned in. "Alone." He huffed rolling his eyes. "Oh yeah, uhm. I guess I will see you in a little bit Ri." He said cautiously bumping into the wall as he went on his way.

His uncle pushed him inside a random room. A frightened man changing his clothes simply stared at the pair confused. "OUT!" His uncle said shouting at him. "But sir I don't have any pants on.". "Everyone down here has a dick in between their legs just like you Emmett!". He quickly scrambled at a pile of unassorted clothes and rushed out of the door trying to cover himself as he went.

"What have you gotten yourself into?" He asked in a loud but hushed tone pushing Rory down to sit in a chair. Rory couldn't open his mouth to speak. His uncle sighed heavily. "You are one lucky bastard. You know that? They were only three names away from the two of you buffoons." His uncle sat down next to him relaxing just a little changing his tone slightly. "Oh Ri... It had to be her? Of all the people as far as your eyes could see." He said still hushed "They would kill you if the King and Queen were to know… It needs to end. NOW Rory.". "I love her Uncle Conn.". "No you don't." he said. "Yes, I do. The same way grandma and grandpa loved each other back in their cottage." Rory stammered. "Oh son, what have you gotten yourself into?" He repeated worriedly looking at his nephew. Rory put his head in his hands leaning on his knees. Conn let out a sigh patting him on the shoulder

"This is only the first of many challenges to come if this is what you choose to proceed with.".

Rory nodded. "Catch back up to Lee.. and Rory.. please be more careful." He said opening the door for him. He looked at Rory's flustered face. Tightening his grip on his shoulder "You need to decide what is best for not only her, but what is best for you." He said letting go and giving him a slight shove out and into the loud and crowded hall. The Captain leaned his weight into the doorframe.

"Sir... May I go in my room now?" Emmet asked holding a two different shirt in front of himself. The captain let out a long laugh "No." he said shutting his door behind him. Emmet look at him afraid and embarrassed. "Emmet. Go put your damn pants on!" He shouted pointing to his room. "Yes sir!" He said confused rushing inside.

He slapped his palm to his forehead taking a deep breath in "May the Gods help us.".

A Violet Night

Chapter 15.)

Violet tightly wound her hair into a bun on top of her head. Without a knock Harriet opened the door. "I see we have new *personal* guards, well done Violet. Well done indeed." Harriet said as she played with Lee's scruffle on his cheeks. She let go of his face and smiled at her cousin "You may stay out here." She said to him as she shut the door in his face. "Indeed." Harriet muttered as she scooted Violet out of the seat at vanity mirror, picking up a red comb with pearls at the base. She brushed her golden blonde locks to the length of her shoulders.

A Violet Night

"Why the long face cousin?" She said continuing to brush through her hair while watching Violets reflection in the mirror behind her. "I laid with Rory last night." Violet said bluntly. Harriet dropped the comb on the table and thrust herself dramatically to turn around in the chair "Violet, why you naughty little harlot.". Violet made a face at her "Was is not pleasureful for you?" She asked smugly "We had sex, and we were caught in the act by a girl. A blast from his past one might say." Violet said sitting on her bed. She wiped her eyes with her palms. She was exhausted. "Well, if she decides to proceed with this information you do have an alibi.". Violet looked at her confused. "Yes... After you spoke with your father you slept in my chambers all night to catch up on the months passed.".

"Thank you." Violet whispered. "After all, no one will believe the words spilled from a peasants mouth. She knows we could have her head for spreading such vile *'lies'* about you." Harriet said standing pointing with the comb, "Now let us go find your lover boy.". "Actually, he is more of a man then you might think." Violet said with a wink and a grin. "Ugh. Now I want details. No actually I take that back I would rather not know." Harriet said with a begging tone.

Violet giggled opening the door for Harriet as she walked out scornfully "Nasty." She whispered to Violet with a grin. "Come now Lee where is your other half." Violet asked. Lee smiled. His white teeth glistened "Late as always, my lady.". He motioned behind her with his hand. She turned around. Rory appeared walking from around the corner of the hall. They both smiled at each other.

"Disgusting." Harriet mumbled under her breath. "Wait, you know?" Lee exclaimed to Harriet sounding relieved "Violet! How many people know about this?" Harriet asked. "Only the two of you." Rory said. "Us, and the whore?" Harriet spat back at him. Lee laughed at her comment. "Yes." Violet whispered not leaving Rory's gaze. "Her name is Visha." Rory said defensive.

"I do believe it's time for breakfast." Lee said clapping his hands together and pointing his fingers down the hall breaking the awkward silence. Rory tilted his hand in the air "After you ladies.".

Violet pulled Rory to the side. "Are we just going to pretend like last night didn't happen? As if that, that whore didn't just interrupt us.". "First of all you don't know her to call her a whore Violet.." He said annoyed grasping her forearm lightly pulling her farther out of sight. "OH, but you do Ri? You seem to care an awful lot about her. Who is she to you?" she said raising her voice. "You need to lower your voice and tread lightly here. She was a friend." He said looking around down the halls. Violet paused as a maid walked past "A friend huh? Friends do not act like that to each other. You must have been screwing her real good for her to cry the way she was over finding us together.".

He sighed taking in what she had said his jaw clenched in annoyance "Yes Violet I have been fucking her. I have been fucking her for years. Is that what you want to hear? That's all she has ever been to me a source of entertainment. I broke thing off with her the day after I kissed you.". "So she just was okay with things ending?" She asked. "If you do not get out of my face with this shit Violet. Of course she was mad about things ending. No she has not stopped trying to contact me, but I keep ignoring her when I see her out and about. I keep my doors locked at night now at night. Which I know you have come to notice. Now look you either trust me or you don't, but I do not want to keep having this conversation with you. I am older than you. I have slept with many other women in my lifetime. You are just going to have to get over it.". Annoyed she pushed his hand off of her forearm. Violet didn't want to talk about the subject with him any longer.

"Get over it Violet and go eat." He said walking ahead of

her. "Ah yes, let us go eat to be someone else's *Source of*

Entertainment." She said speed walking past him. Rory

raised his hands in confusion and anger "What are you even

saying anymore?". She shrugged her shoulders "I suppose

you wouldn't understand now would you.". He looked at

her rubbing his eye with his hand.

Violet could not escape all of the thoughts gushing

through her mind. Her once beautiful night was tainted of

flash images across her mind. Rory and Visha entangled

sharing the bed, and more than likely the same sheets they

laid on together. They were two completely different

spectrums on a scale.

They could not begin to compare to one another,

and this racked her brain. Not even similar in looks, so how

could she even be in his sights? Violet began to become

insecure with her thoughts.

A Violet Night

Harriet set her glass of water down. A 'clank' broke the silence in the room. Violets eyes came back into focus. Rory and Lee began to stiffen their posture at the end of the table.

"Good morning." He fathers voice called out from behind her. "Beautiful morning to you as well uncle." Harriet said wiping her mouth with the napkin that was placed neatly in her lap. She stood up to great him.

Violet stood up as well doing her best not to look at Rory. She didn't want to see him. She couldn't. All she saw when she looked at him was him doing all of their moments with someone else.

Violet turned around locking eyes with not only her father but Niran as well. He smiled at her hugely showing his teeth. "Good morning father." She said lowly. "You are not going to great our new commander?" Her father said excitedly. "Oh Niran! How excited you must be!" Harriet said swooping to his side. He looked at her excepting the moment, before peeling her off of his arm "Yes, how exciting indeed!" He exclaimed looking around the room at everyone.

"Are these the brave souls you entrusted to guard your finest treasures?" He said looking at her father astonished. "Indeed!" He said proudly shoving his chest out slightly.

"Well, do introduce me Violet I would love to meet the fine men!" He said reaching onto the table for a toothpick. The way he said her name ran her blood cold. She was frozen. Harriet looked at her confused and scowled. She moved past Violet bumping into her softly as she went. She grabbed his arm again and walked over to the pair across the room.

He studied them over them trying to contain his laughter. Violet looked at Rory's expressionless face. "Fine men indeed Farris!" He said picking lent off of Rory's shoulder. She looked back at her father, grinning ear to ear as if it was his idea to have them guard the two. He cleared his throat. "Come son. I need to have a rest." He said waving him to come along. "I'll be right behind you!" Niran said still smiling looking deep into Rory's eyes. The king chuckled "Don't stay too long down here or I may be asleep when you return to the command table.". "Farris you are always asleep at the command table." He joked back to her father while they exchanged laughter.

After his footsteps turned into silence Niran leaned into Rory's left ear "Good to see you again friend.". He shot eyes at Violet as if he was going to say something else "I best be on my way, you heard your father." He straightened up Rory's shirt.

He paused, and with every ounce of energy he had in his body he jumped towards Lee stomping his foot in front of him. Caught off guard Lee jumped backwards nearly stumbling to catch his bearings. Niran became

hysterical with laughter "Oh that is grand" he wiped a tear

from his eye "They could not save a fish from water… I'll

be seeing you around my ladies." He kissed Harriet's hand,

and then reached for Violets. She snatched it back closer to

her chest. He smiled again at her and then looked back at

Rory. "I suppose I will be seeing all of you around." He

said moving his toothpick around with his tongue. He

dismissed himself with a low chuckle from his throat.

"I could have taken him!" Lee said reassuring

Harriet. She looked back at him pulling her top lip up and

scrunching her brow "How embarrassed you must be.".

"He just got the best of me honest! I was too invested in the

weird interest he has in you." Lee said to Rory who stayed

silent looking up at Violet. "He's irrelevant here." Violet

said matching Rory's attitude towards the group.

"You know Ann would have loved to see this."

Harriet said in a sudden sadden tone. She grabbed her

cousins arm in comfort, "But I am happy we have gotten closer Violet. You are not the brat I thought you were.". Violet rolled her eyes with smiled annoyed "Thank you Harriet.". "Oh. Don't go getting mushy on me now." Harriet said sucking her tears back up. "Wouldn't dream of it" she said pushing her cousin away with a disgruntled laugh.

A Violet Night

<u>Chapter 16.)</u>

Five months came and went as fast as the sun and moon interchange. "Come, I want to show you something." Rory said with a smile. He grabbed Violet by the hand pulling her alongside him.

Once they entered the tree line he slowed his pace. "What is it?" She asked eagerly. He put his finger to her lips with a mischievous grin "It's a surprise.". She watched the excitement flood his face making herself smile.

Following him deeper into the woods on a thin walked path "There." He said pointing into the treetops "Remember this tree". Tied to a branch was a dirty old red handkerchief. He pulled it down stuffing it into his pocket leading her off the path. She looked around taking in the images of her surroundings. With the path no more the deep green abyss filled growing ever larger with thorny bushes, and tall overgrown weeds that brushed against her.

"Come on Ri. Where are we going?" She begged tugging on his hand like a child. He ignored her and continued walking. Pushing branches and thorn bushes out of the way for them with the heels of his black boots.

"Listen." He said breaking the silence. They paused; she could hear faint running water. They came upon the bottom of s rock cliff covered in moss, vines, and leaves. "A dead end?" She asked amused. Rory moved the leaves and branches out of the way to reveal a small rock door. To the eye it was nearly invisible.

He rolled it opened it for her "Only the finest go first." He insisted. Violet crouched her head down to enter. She regained her posture dodging the webs that hung low.

The smell of moist earth filled her nose. It was dark on the other side. Pitch black when Rory closed the door. She grabbed his arm as he chuckled. "Scared?" He asked. "What is this place?" She asked tightening her grip. His ears remained deaf to her questioning.

They continued down a straight chilled path until they bumped into another door. Rory opened the wooden door. It creaked open slowly revealing the inside of a small cottage. With the sun pouring in through the thin wooden slats on two of the walls the opposites were an old dingy stone, and a small blue stain glass window right above the door. Across from them she could see a bed in one corner and a rocking chair in the other. On the stone wall next to where they entered was a tiny fireplace just large enough for one pot or so. The sound of running water was roaring now. "Where are we?" Violet whispered in awe touching a small trinket on a table on the other side of her. "This. This is my hideaway." He said walking towards the other door, slowly he opened it revealing the most beautiful landscape she had ever seen.

A waterfall that emerged from the rocks above made it look as if heaven itself had open wide. Pooling at the bottom into a clear creek bed with the most beautiful stones of all colors gleaming at underneath the water. "It is beautiful!" She gasped amazed.

He smiled watching her take it all in "Yes it is." He reassured. She felt her cheeks begin to blush . She hugged him tightly around his neck pulling him down to her height. He wrapped his arms around her holding her tighter giving her a kiss on the side of her head. Rory pulled away from her with excitement on his face "Wait here!".

Rory ran into the cottage coming back out with a dusty old blue and white checkered quilt. He sat on his knees next to the large flat stone in the ground. Carefully he unwrapped the quilt revealing a smaller cloth which he laid in the center. Within the small cloth revealed grapes, different cheeses, meats, a loaf of bread, and a small bottle of wine with two beautiful crystal chalices.

"You did not have to do all of this! Where did you get all of this?" she said sitting next to him placing her hand on his. "I stole it." Rory said tearing the bread into two halves. Violet rolled her eyes and tried not to laugh "Oh, you thought that was a joke." Rory said letting out a laugh. She looked at him concerned. "Relax. The merchant was a crook for his prices." Violet took a bite of the bread and looked away. "Loosen up. That is how the real world works outside of your walls princess. It's eat or be eaten out here.". "Shut up." Violet said annoyed giving him a kick with her foot. "And these glasses come from the finest craftsmanship.. Straight out of your cupboard.". "Ah, I did think they looked vaguely familiar." She said raising her glass for him to fill.

A Violet Night

Rory let out a sigh then stood up beginning to take off his clothes, everything except his briefs. "Now what are you doing?" She asked curiously. He waded his way into the creek "What does it look like I'm doing." He said sarcastically. "Don't be an ass Rory." She said intrigued taking a drink of wine out of the bottle. "I'm sorry did you say something?" he asked as he splashed water at her. "Well come on, don't be a Harriet now." He said diving in coming back up using both of his hands to wipe his face and push his hair back.

Violet took another sip of the wine and shed her dress. Standing on the bank in her white slip she let the cold water wash over her feet. She bit her lip and walked in the water, wading out to Rory. He was taken back watching her come towards him. Watching her round breast bounce with every step she took. As the water splashed higher it made her white slip transparent and fused with her skin so tight he could see every bit of her hard nipples through it.

He caught his breath. She wrapped her legs around him. They began to kiss passionately. She could feel him get harder the more they kissed. Rory ran his fingers through her hair drifting one hand around her bottom and the other on her breast.

Rory carried her back to shore. The water poured off of their chilled skin. Still carrying her he struggled to bust through the door to the cottage. Their breathing grew heavier as he laid her down on the bed. Taking off her slip and his briefs he kissed every inch of her body making each of her thighs shake in the process before he entered her. He grabbed her hands pinning them down with their fingers interlocked.

Laying on his bare chest Violet made circles with her finger on his arm. "Rory?" She asked. He looked down at her. "I think I love you with more than love." She said. Her heart began to beat a little faster. "That's funny." He said laying his arm around her. Violets heart sank in her chest. "That's funny, because I know I love you." He said kissing her head. "Don't do that to me!" She said with a laugh. He smiled greatly as he gave her a squeeze.

Rory got up and exited the cottage once more. He could feel her eyes on him walking away. Violet looked around soaking in all of the raw energy from the moment.

Rory handed Violet her dress. She grabbed it and slipped it back on without the wet slip. She hung the slip in the windowsill. Violet looked into the mirror to take the pins out of her hair. He smiled to himself gliding into his pants.

He looked up to the sky clouds were gathering and he could smell rain in the air. He looked back at Violet in the doorway and smiled to himself as she wrang out her long hair. It dripped on her bare feet.

He walked back to her holding her in his embrace "This is such a lovely place Ri." She said looking up at him rubbing her hand up his chest. "It's even more lovely now that it is 'OUR' place." He said giving her a kiss on the forehead. *"Our place."* Violet said to herself. She couldn't help but smile at that sound of the words coming out of his mouth.

She gripped his hand slightly tighter. He squeezed back smiling at her. She leaned her head onto his chest listening to his fast heartbeat hit her ears like pounding drums.

A Violet Night

<u>Chapter 17.)</u>

Thunder rumbled in the distance. Finding their way back to the path "We need to hurry." Rory said grasping for her hand as he quickened his pace looking up at the darkening sky. "Think of all the questions we would raise." She said tapping her chin with her index finger. He pulled her forward lightly with a grin.

"Let go of me!" A voice screamed from up the pathway. Rory put his arm in front of Violet and put his finger to his lips to silence her from saying anymore "Stay here." He whispered placing Violet behind a tree. She crossed her arms. He silently walked just on the inside of the tree line slowly approaching the muffled argument.

"Times up girl. The money was due last week." An older man said grabbing a small brunette girl by her wrist. "I said, let me go!" The girl shouted swatting at his face with her free hand. He let out an annoyed laugh leaning back to dodge her. He lifted his hand and punched her in the chest knocking her to the ground. Rory could feel the connection as the mans' fist made impact. He took a couple steps closer to the dispute. The rain pitter pattered off of Rory's shoulders.

She didn't let out a single cry. The girl held her chest trying to catch her breath. The man took a step forward as she kicked him as hard as she could in the knee bending it backwards. A bone snapping 'crack' filled the air. The man howled out in pain falling down to the wet ground. She stood up wiping the rain from her face into the collar of her shirt. He swung at her again stumbling to stand up with his good leg. Shifting all of her weight kicking him again in this time in the throat knocking him back down into the mud.

"My father's debt to you is not of my own." She said watching him struggle to catch his breath while he grabbed at his throat with his short fat fingers gasping for air. "I should have- *Wheeze* just- *Wheeze* sold your ass to the whore house when I had the chance." He said looking up at her coughing. The girl reached down around her ankle and pulled a dagger from her boot. "And I should leave you to bleed out on this road." She said tracing the blade from her index finger down to his nose swiftly in one motion.

Rory jumped as he felt Violets arm touch his. "We have to do something." She whispered in his ear "We have to help her.". "Violet I do not think she needs our help." He said as they continued to watch from the sidelines.

A Violet Night

"Piece of shit." She mumbled "Take out all of the money you have.". "You are insane!" He said trying to swing on her again. She swung the dagger cutting his forearm. "Bitch!" He slurred grabbing his arm tightly with the other arm falling onto the ground in front of him. She looked at him placing one foot on his back. Reaching down into his pocket she pulled out a small green leather bag. The girl shifted its weight in her palm tossing the bag in the air with a smile before placing it into her own pocket. "Better get crawling. It's a long way home uncle... You don't want to be out here when the storm picks up." She said pointing the blade down the trail looking at it eye level.

Thunder crackled in the sky. The girl looked up to the clouds and put her hood up on her cloak. She took off running farther down the path.

Rory and Violet looked at each other "What was that?" She asked. Rory shook his head and laughed uneasy

"I really don't know, but we're not going to confrontate.".
He grabbed her hand again pulling her passed the man in
the path groaning in agony begging for the pair to stop and
help him. Violet looked at him with compassion slowing
her pace as they walked. Rory shook his head at her sternly
and pulled her along. She watched over her shoulder while
he screamed vulgarly at them.

The treetops above rustled, "Why are you
following me?". They looked up. The girl perched in the
branches holding her dagger now pointing it down at them.
"What? No." Violet said.

The girl jumped down. Rory drew his sword
halfway. "No." Violet said putting her hand on his "We
don't know her story.". "I restate my question. Who are
you two and why are you following me?" she asked again.
"My name is Violet. And this is Rory." She said politely.

A Violet Night

The girl began to chuckle to herself "Princesses Violet.". She tossed her hands up playfully threading the dagger in between her fingers. Rory looked at her harshly and cleared his throat. Her laugh faded as her eyes darted back and forth from Rory to Violet.

"Princess." The girl said shocked. She dropped to her knees putting the dagger away "Please forgive my tongue your highness.". "Stand. You need not kneel in my presents." Violet said holding her hand out to help the girl up. "Vi. Do you think that's a good idea?" Rory whispered to her "Hush." Violet extending her arm farther. Cautiously the girl reached for her hand letting her pull her up. "What's your name love?" Violet asked still holding the girls hand.

"Scarlet." She whispered, "From whom do you hail?" Violet asked, "Mother has never been around, my father is dead, and my sister was sold to the whore house years ago. The last I heard she had passed from an illness, choking on blood in her sleep.". "How old are you?" Violet asked searching her eyes. "16. Well I will be 16 in the upcoming weeks".

Violet patted her hand and turned and beginning to walk to Rory, "We have to take her back with us." She whispered to Rory. "No. No way in the hell are you taking her back with you. Do you really think she won't play you the way she did that man back there? We do not know if that was really her uncle.".

"To be fair he deserved it, and he was my uncle. My father barrowed a lot of money from him To pay he sold my older sister when she passed away he lost his way in the bottle and picked the wrong tavern fight." Scarlet said butting into their conversation taking a step forward with her hands behind her back.

They looked back at her together. He put his hand up to halt her, "Violet no.". "Well come on then." Violet said turning back around waving her forward. "I don't want your pity princess. No offense." Scarlet said looking at Rory. "I said lets go. You will come, you will bathe, eat a hot meal then you can decide what you want to do from there.".

She looked at Violet before her eyes softened and nodded her head. Rory looked at Violet dumbfounded. Violet shrugged her shoulders "Are you not glad your uncle brought you to us?" she asked him. "Violet that is completely different.". "No good deed goes unnoticed Rory." She said watching the girls' body weight shift with curiosity as she quickly walked up to the pair.

Rory put his hand on Scarlets shoulder and put his other hand out palm side up looking down at her dagger. "Really?" She asked annoyed. He continued to stare at her silently. She rolled her eyes reaching down and placing it into his hand. He tightened his grip on her. "Come on!" She said handing him a longer blade in a sheath from her pants.

He pushed her forward. Violet looked at him shaking her head. "It is still my job to keep you safe *princess*." He said tucking her daggers away in his satchel.

They made their way back to Violets chambers. "Behind those doors you can draw yourself a bath, and in those drawers you can find night clothes. I will bring you a hot meal when you have finished.. Oh, and do not leave this room without me." Scarlet thanked her.

"This is a mistake Violet. At the least make her rest in another room." He worried. "Enough. Then let it be my own mistake.". "You are stubborn you know that?" he said giving her a kiss on the forehead. She smiled "I know.". He scoffed at her shaking his head nervously. "We will be okay." She assured. "I'm not worried about her." He said looking past her as the Scarlet looked around the room awestruck. She smiled and patted his chest shutting the door behind her.

A Violet Night

Chapter 18.)

Violet let Rory pull out her chair. She sat at the table across from her mother, father, Niran sat at his left side and Harriet next to him. Everyone had already begun to eat without her.

Violet placed her napkin in her lap noticing that tonight her father looked very sweaty and pale "Late again?" Her mother asked putting her fork to her pink lips without looking up. She pretended as if she didn't hear her. She watched her mother chew her meat slowly.

A Violet Night

"You may go." Her father motioned Rory and Lee to leave. They silently bowed their heads and left the room.

She watched them leave looking back at her mother who was staring her down hard. Violet dipped her fingertips in the water bowl and dried them off. She picked at the meal in front of her too anxious to eat. She watched as they all enjoyed their food talking amongst themselves with smiles. She avoided eye contact with Niran when she could, but she could still feel his eyes on her.

"Where have you been lately?" He father asked. "I-" Violet began as she looked at Harriet for help who slightly shook her head no with wide eyes. He looked at her reluctantly chewing his last bite. She stopped herself from finishing her sentence. *"He knows."* She thought to herself. Violet sat up stiff in her chair her heart racing in the pit of her chest.

A Violet Night

"I have been taking walks outside of the walls...
Guarded!.. Guarded of course father." She spoke. Her
father paused after wiping his mouth with the cloth napkin
that was in his lap. "I know." He said "I wanted to see if
you would tell me the truth Violet. Which leads me to ask
you my dear daughter.. You would tell me if someone has
made advances towards you wouldn't you?".

Harriet chocked on her water. Coughing and
looking around she mumbled "I am so sorry. I think this is
a conversation for just you all to have without me. If I may
I be excused Uncle?". Her father without taking his eyes
off of Violet unfolded his hands and waved her on. She
looked at Niran who gave her a wink as he chewed his meat
silently with a grin.

"Of course I would." She said swallowing hard as
her stomach sank. He blankly stared at her nodding his
head running his tongue against his teeth under his lips "I

see..." He began coughing loudly pulling the napkin again to his mouth.

"Are you alright?" She asked standing up to assist her father hoping it would shift the conversation differently. He raised his hand as she approached. Niran put his hand on her father's back. She could see dark blood inside of it as he wadded it up quickly pulling it out of her view.

"Finish your food. Elda worked hard on that for you." He said trying to find his voice once more. She stood there watching him as a drop of sweat beaded down his forehead. He motioned to the captain who was standing in the corner overseeing. Niran abandon the rest of his meal and helped him find his footing to stand. Together the three of them walked down the hall. Her father taking a moment to lean against it and then resumed walking.

"You should go to bed as well if you are not going to eat." Her mother said now too standing with both of her hands folded in front of her midline "It's going to be a long day tomorrow for you Violet.".

Violet helped clear the dishes with Elda bringing them back to the kitchen and placing them onto the countertop where three other women took them to be washed.

"What's that supposed to mean? It's going to be a long day tomorrow?" Violet pondered as she poured a hot bowl of stew and placed it on the metal tray with a couple rolls. "Violet! I do believe I have already served you tonight, and I do not recall you ever coming for seconds unless it was for pastries." Elda's voice broke through her concentration. Pushing her thoughts out of her mind Violet told Elda about Scarlet hiding in her room.

A Violet Night

"And this street girl is just hauled up in your room?" Elda asked concerned raising her brow at her. "Well, I hope she still is." Violet joked as they walked up the stairs and down the hall to her room. "I hope she didn't steal anything or make a mess." Elda said opening the door.

A cleaned-up Scarlet with hair soaking wet around her shoulders sat in front of the mirror. Her eyes were pink and puffy. She had been crying. "Are you alright?" Violet asked confused and concerned setting the tray down. "Why did you do this for me?" Scarlet asked with a sniffle. "I would want someone to do the same for me. Also it is better to have friends then enemies." Violet said scooting the tray in front of her. Placing her hand on Scarlets shoulder. "You may stay here as long as you would like as my guest, and maybe one day hopefully as my friend..". "Thank you your highness." She said with a smile.

"If you're going to stay here, you may call me Violet just as everyone else does." She said with a grin. "First thing in the morning we will find you an appropriate new wardrobe." Elda said picking up her raggedy brown blouse and blue pants off of the floor "And we'll burn this."

They all shared a laughed together. "I think you have all been locked away too long up here. Didn't you know this is the latest out there." Scarlett joked with Elda. "Oh honey, if this is the latest I'd hate to see what else is coming." She said worried.

Elda pulled Violet aside as Scarlett went to lay down "Violet-" "I know, I know. This was reckless, but she deserves a chance." Violet said waiting to be scolded. "I was going to tell you I am so very proud of you and who you are becoming." She said quietly with a grin before giving her a long hug "Do not let this world change who you are Violet." She whispered in her ear "There is not enough good anymore.". Violet nodded her head.

A Violet Night

She followed Elda out into the hall until they split their directions for the evening. Violet stopped at Harriet's chambers. Without knocking she walked inside. The blankets flew up over her chest "Is there no privacy?!" She shouted at her. Niran poked his head up from beside her. He waved at Violet with a crooked smile "Would you like to join us?" He asked playfully. She left abruptly closing the door listening to their muffled laughs from the other side of the doorframe. Violet shivered and shook her to each side.

She wondered the halls walking past her mother and fathers chambers. She listened to him cough as it echoed throughout the hallways. "Excuse me miss." A doctor said as he pulled his black elongated mask over his slender face. He smelled of vinegar and peppermint oils. He readjusted his black leather gloves that stretched to his forearms. She slid out of his way so he could pull open the door.

A Violet Night

Chapter 19.)

"The captain sends word for us." Lee said leaning into Rory's room. "Okay?" Rory confusedly laughed. He stopped shining his shoes tossing his rag onto the table. Lee remained silent. Rory felt his tension growing. His smile slid from his cheeks meeting his friends gaze.

Walking into the meeting hall they took their place in a line of men. Rory's stomach flipped inside out. "Now that you are all here. The king has specially requested this group of young men into the next line of battle... I know that this is not what you wanted to hear this early in your day, but the time has come to honor your King and your kingdom." The captain said looking directly at Rory. They could feel air around them become dense. "What is he talking about?" Lee whispered to Rory frantically "I thought we were protected?". *"Me too."* He thought to himself *"Me too."*.

"Alright get packing boys we leave tomorrow. So I suggest you make the most out of the hours you have left today. Say your goodbyes. Make your peace. Runners will. Be. Captured and killed on sight." Captain said watching the men file out of the room in silence.

Rory stayed behind as Lee lingered in the doorway. "This has to be a mistake." He said. His uncle paused before taking out a small scroll setting it on the table he ran his finger down to the bottom of the list he said "Guerrero, Rory. I do believe that is you boy. You must have pissed someone off terribly to go from where you were to here... I was handed this this morning.".

A Violet Night

Rory's heart sank lower in his chest reading his own name and Lee's below. He nodded his head walking out of the room. Lee followed "So what did he say?". "Lee we are on that list. In fact we're the last two names on there. Fresh ink.". "You do not think that-" Rory cut him off "Oh but I do." He said, "He knows.".

Instead of packing right away he needed some air, alone. Sitting down against the outside garden wall Rory sat on the ground reevaluating his life. The sound of rustling in the weeds startled him.

He looked over now standing in a defensive position. A medium sized tan with black spots, blue eyed dog emerged panting heavily. He let out a smile shifting his weight to crouch down "Come here, it's alright." He snapped his fingers motioning to dog. It cocked its head to the side letting its tongue roll out. Rory sat back down and shook his head "I don't know what to do." He said out loud letting his head hit the wall behind him.

A Violet Night

Beginning to zone off yet again staring at the ground where the blades of grass met the clover patches. He let the loose soil embed in between his open fingers.

The panting grew louder. Now in his right ear he turned his head to be met with the sour smell of dog breath. The dog sat at his side and laid down next to him with a grunt.

Rory placed his hand on the dogs head and began to pet it. The dog rolled over. "You like that huh girl?" He said with a smile. The drool ran down her jaws and into her wrinkles. *"What is a nanny dog doing out here?"*. "You're all bones girl." He said rubbing his hands over her rib cage.

Finding his footing again Rory started to walk behind him into the garden. He looked back expecting to see the dog. He felt something bump his knee out of the way. He turned his attention below. The dog had not only followed him but was now tucked in between his legs looking up at him. Her tongue, and drool flopping in the wind. He smiled down at her. Scrunching her face in his hands.

He snuck in the kitchen window and grabbed a cut slab of meat curing. Elda looked up from her work and looked at him disappointingly. He cheekily smiled at her, waving, then disappearing back through the window. "Dumb boy." He heard Elda say to herself under her breath. He raced with the dog weaving in and out of his legs until he got back to his spot against the wall.

He tore a small piece off for himself and held the larger piece out for the dog. She took it in her mouth and sat at his feet gnawing at it quickly. When she sat he noticed a scar on her back. "You are a tough girl aren't you?" He said running his fingers over the bumpy scar. The dog shook, then went back to eating. "Pierced by an arrow and yet still walking around.".

Wheels started to turn in his head "And Arrow you shall be." Her tail began to wag as she looked up at him. "You like that name?" he leaned down and scratched behind her ears with both of his hands "You deserve a tough name for such a tough girl.".

"Rory." A voice rang out through the tree line across the way. His body stiffened up "Please go away." He said not wanting to turn his head. "Rory please listen to me. It is important.". He sighed turning around to see Visha walking slowly towards him. Arrow ran to her and then back to him laying again at his feet. She smiled but let it fade quickly from her lips. "I want you to know that what is happening is not because of me.".

"Oh, okay. Like I should believe that… Because I am just supposed to trust you after…?... Why would you ever have any say in something with the higher ups?" He asked staring straight into her eyes. She broke eye contact and began bawling her fist up at her waistline walking

within arm's reach of him she pointed in his face "I am not
the one you should be talking to about trust Rory! I loved
you, and you said you loved me too! I was there for you for
so many things until..".

"Until what?" He said angrily shoving her hand
down. "You know exactly what happened!.. SHE
happened! You found something new and exciting and
dropped me in the dust." Visha exclaimed. "What are you
even talking about?" He shouted throwing his hands up in
the air.

"You met her and forgot all about me! I turn the
corner and you walk the other way. I come to see you and
the doors are locked. I ask Lee about you, and it is nothing
except secrecy.. YOU broke me Rory!". "I figured you got
my hints." He said trying to ignore her words. Visha
nodded her head taking a deep breath "You know what?
It's fine Ri. Just forget it. You will see my warnings soon

enough.". "What is that supposed to mean?" He asked as she began to walk off.

"You'll see Rory. Don't say I did not try to tell you first." She said waving her hand in the air at him. "She is crazy." He said out loud looking down at Arrow. Visha smiled angrily at him turning and continuing to walk away.

He watched her leave. He shook his head again in disbelief "See now what did I tell you she's crazy". The dog cocked her head at him. "Oh alright." He said tossing her his meat also. She caught it in her mouth and chewed heavily.

He looked back up, but she was already long gone. He squinted his eyes trying to look farther for her. "C'mon girl. I have someone I'd like you to meet." He said looking up one more time to see if Visha had come back.

A Violet Night

Chapter 20.)

A knock at the door awoke Scarlet. She looked

outside the sun was barely in the sky and then shook Violet.

Rory walked halfway into the doorway. Violet sat up

covering her mouth with one hand to yawn "You're

awfully early." she said sleepily "May we have a moment?"

He said darting eyes between the girls. She smiled at

Scarlet. Who nodded and stood up looking around the

room. "There should be clothes in there." Violet said

pointing. Scarlett nodded closing the door behind her to the

privy.

A Violet Night

"Close your eyes." He demanded playfully. Doing what she was told she covered her eyes with her hands while smiling. She glanced through the slits in her fingers. "No peaking!" He shouted. "No fun!" Violet grinned. The door closed behind him. She could hear a heavy pitter patter of footsteps and a sudden flop on the bed. "Open them." He said proudly.

A beautiful dog tan with the bluest eyes she had ever seen on an animal sat next to her. She got up off the bed and hugged the dog petting her all over "What is this?" she asked surprised. "A present. A guardian for when I am not with you… I've taken the liberty to name her Arrow.". "A beautiful name really!" She said as Arrow licked her cheek. Her smile dissipated "You are my guardian always Ri." She said reaching for his hand. "I can't always be with you Violet. This way I know you will always be safe." He said so desperately wanting to tell her the truth.

Elda interrupted with a knock and walked into the room pausing at the two and the dog "My stew meat better not have gone to this mutt." She scolded pointing at Rory. Violet looked at them puzzled. "It's a long story." He responded. "No it is not. He stole my meat." Elda snared turning her attention to Violet, "Your father is calling for you by name." She shifted her tone. "My father?" She asked. Elda sucked in her bottom lip and nodded her head slowly.

"Go. I will be here for you when you get back." He said reassuring her. She quickly changed out of her yellow nightgown and into something more appropriate. Closing the door behind them Violet asked, "How bad is he?".

With all of the subtle hints over the past few months Violet had known that her father was sick. She had simply put it out of her mind because people get sick all the time and are always fine soon enough after. Elda stayed silent looking ahead as they continued to walk. Violet felt her throat become tight as she tried to swallow. She crossed her arms trying to embrace herself. Elda reached over and placed her hand on the back of her upper arm rubbing it softly.

Stopping at the door Elda paused looking at Violet, her eyes saddened and heavy "I know you two never saw eye to eye with one another, but he is still your father and somewhere in his heart he loves you.. Not more then I love you of course." She paused to place her hand on her cheek ".. But more or less of the same my dear.". She let out a sigh placing her palm on the door "Violet he's dying. This is it.".

A whirl wind of emotions flew through Violets body as the doors to her fathers' chambers opened slowly. Everyone in the room turned their attention to her. She drug her feet inside. The room smelled sweet as the aroma of death filled her nose. Men and women alongside her mother and Harriet crowded around the canopy topped bed.

A Violet Night

The emerald curtains on the bed were all closed but on the right side they had been left open.

She took a deep breath and walked to the bed standing behind her mother who sat emotionless, and Harriet who sat alongside holding her hands in her lap. Across the room Niran had a nervous look on his face with his hands behind his head leaning against the wall. His eyes darted to Violet filled with empathy. She could tell he had been crying. Violet turned her attention to her father.

Her father's breathing was labored. He was so pale and was wheezing his hardest. Violet sat on the side of the bed taking her father's hand in her own. She could feel her face begin to heat up as she fought back the tears welling in her eyes.

His eyes normally brown fluttered open. They were glazed over bloodshot with a silver brown color. He began to cough heavily. Violet reached over to the nightstand picking up a white napkin and placed it in his hands.

He lowered his hands to the bed revealing the napkin now filled with blood. He began to wheeze again "Violet," he whispered painfully through the gasps. She leaned in closer "I'm right here daddy." She said squeezing his hand now on his chest. "I wish to talk with my daughter alone." He said hushed. Violet looked to the captain at the foot of the bed as he began to usher everyone out of the room quickly and quietly.

Her father pushed up with his elbows weakly letting the rag on his forehead tumble off and onto the bed. He pointed to the table. Violet brought the small glass of water up to his lips and helped him sit up the rest of the way.

She could tell it was taking his all to sit up like this, sweat now poured down his temples. She grabbed the rag that had left a small wet ring on the sheets and wiped the beads of sweat dripping from his brow.

"Violet. I have but very few hours left in this world, and when I'm gone… I want you to be safe." he paused "But daddy I am safe." She said reassuringly patting his hand and placing the glass back down on the table. He laid back on his propped up pillows squeezing her hands weakly. "That is why you are to wed Niran tomorrow.". Violet dropped his hands. "W-what?" She gasped jumping up off of the bed.

He coughed some more as the pain in his eyes grew. Violet stood there dumbfoundedly blinded by this information. "You will need a good man Violet. You will need a strong king to lead beside you. Now I know this is hard for you because of your sister, but it is what is best for the kingdom.".

A Violet Night

"I won't." She whispered still in shock. "Even on my death bed my daughter you are as defiant as ever… You will marry him. End of discussion. It is what is best.". "For whom father?" she asked raising her voice. "For the kingdom Violet. Since the day you took your first breath this life has never been about you. As a queen soon you will understand that.". "I do not love him!" she wrenched heartbroken. "In time you will love him Violet. You have no say in this." he said watching his daughter begin to turn her back to him.

"… He was no good for you Violet. You have to know that.." He said catching her off guard. "Who?" She asked, her heart beating wildly like a drum in her chest. He looked at her sternly "I am no idiot Violet. I can see the way you look at him. No one had to tell me anything I didn't already know.".

Violet made her way to the door fighting back tears. "You cannot run from this my child. This is what you were meant to do. Please do not let my cry fall upon deaf ears. Accept this.." He said weakly. Violet paused before slamming open the doors. The crowed that had all been eves dropping at the door leaped back to evade getting hit. Harriet looked at her with confusion. She reached for her cousin who shoved her away harshly.

Violet felt sick, everything around her was closing in around her. Quickly she sat in the middle of the hallway while the guest walked around her to reenter the chamber. Harriet reached for her again this time with more aggression. Violet fought it for a second before giving up.

"How could he?" She whispered as the dam of tears burst from her eyes. Harriett began stroking her hair looking up at Niran confused. He kneeled down to their level. Violet buried her face into her cousins neck and shoulder grabbing onto her tightly drenching her with tears. He went in with his hand to rub the back of her head but withdrew his it and stood back up.

A Violet Night

Violet turned her head. Her mother who had been watching from down the hall had become one with the stone making eye contact solely with her daughter.

"How could you let him do this to me?!" She howled in pain. Her mother with empty eyes walked past her and back into the room with Niran escorting her. He looked back at Violet and watched as began to hyperventilate clutching Harriet making her knuckles turn white.

Violet couldn't breathe she was choking on her own tears into Harriet's shoulder. "Shhh.. there, there." She whispered, "Breathe Violet just breathe.". she said holding her head close to her body. She wanted to scream. Fill her lungs to the brink of them exploding and just scream, but nothing came out.

"It shocked me too when Niran told me last night." She said quietly. Violets body began to shake. "It is going to be okay. He's a good man Violet. You will see." She said smiling "I am proud to have lost him to you. Now come let's get you all cleaned up. These people are far to nosey, and you have an image to preserve." she said pealing her head off of her.

Elda came up beside them helping to pull Violet to her feet. They walked her arm in arm back to her room "I've got it from here." She said nodding at her cousin and to Elda. Harriet forced another fake smile and nodded back to her. Elda patted her hand "I am right here for you baby." She said. "I know." She said leaning so Elda could kiss her cheek.

A Violet Night

<u>Chapter 21.)</u>

Violet opened the door to her room her face red and sore from crying. Her head pounding as loud as ever. "Out." She scorned to Scarlet watching Rory play with Arrow on her bed. "You knew." She whispered angrily. "I found out I was leaving this morning." He said still playing with Arrow not wanting to look up at her angry gaze.

"Leaving? Going where?" She asked confused. He looked up at her confused "I am going to war in the morning Violet. Your father put both Lee's name and my own on the list last night.".

A Violet Night

She began to cry again sitting on the edge of the bed. "I am to wed Niran in the morning.". "What? He can't do that." He said crawling to the end of the bed to embrace her. "He can, and he is." She parted through her tears.

"Runaway with me." He said taking her by the arms. "Violet runaway with me. We can start a new life together. With you as my wife we can see the world together and get out of this hell.".

As amazing as that sounded to her ears she let her small smile slide off of her face. "We mustn't. A life of running is no life at all. Not to mention if Niran has us captured it would be both of our heads." She laid her head on his shoulder, "You have a better chance at living if you leave tomorrow Ri. We both know it.". "What about you?" He asked forcefully facing her "What kind of a life will you have with that monster?". "Not the life I want, but a life none the less. I will be fine Ri, I have Elda, Scarlett, and now Arrow. Maybe Harriet too once she sets aside her own feelings.".

Rory paused pushing her hair behind her ears, and wiping the tears from her eyes "Violet, I will come back for you. We can live at the waterfall in the cottage alone. No one will ever find us there. We just need to buy a little time to build up supplies.". She smiled at him "I can stage my death and hide at cottage waiting for you, but Ri you will have to stay alive for me.". "Trust me, not even death could tear us apart." He said taking her face in his hands and kissing her slowly "I will always find my way back to you.". She believed him with every inch of her being.

Rory stood up locking the door and coming back to her he shoved her back on the bed taking off his shirt. Violet pulled him back on top of her kissing him passionately. There on her bed, they made love as if it was the first and last time they would ever do it again.

A Violet Night

They did not eat or sleep all day or night, but instead laid there with each other dreaming up plans for their cottage. How she would make her death look realistic.

"Are you going to be okay?" He asked, "Only for a little while of course.". "I survived long before I stumbled into you Rory do not forget this prison has always been my home." She joked. "Some days I am unsure who has the most tragic backstory between our lives." He said putting his hand behind his head to prop it up.

"Personally I do believe Lee has to have the most recent tragedy." She said. "How so?" He asked. "He has been stuck to Harriet's side all this time. I am surprised he has not lost his mind." She laughed. "Ironically, I do believe they balance each other out pretty well." He said smiling at her watching the lights dance in her eyes.

"Violet?" he said softly. "Yes Rory?" She answered. He softly placed her hand to his cheek looking deeply into her eyes "Somedays I think back, and I am ashamed of how I was before I met you." He said shyly. She took a moment to respond "We are who we are. We bring out different versions of ourselves around certain people. Though, we never truly change ourselves for someone else we simply mask the worst for someone new.". "I do not believe for one moment that you would have liked me." He said. "Perhaps, perhaps not. We are now who we are together not who we were before." She said bringing their foreheads together. He kissed her nose and then pecked at her lips.

They never wanted to forget how each other looked at this very moment in time. The way every source of light seemed to make a spotlight for them to see each other and entangle themselves even farther.

They watched the sun come up together lying naked on a blanket on the balcony floor. Rory balled up his fist tapping it lightly on the ground beside his thigh and the floor. She watched him fidget, as she did so on his chest tracing her hand up and down "I am not ready to spend a day without you here." She whispered kissing his shoulder smelling his masculine scent.

He took her hand into his "I know." He said kissing the top of her hand. "I will be back for you Violet. That I can promise you.". "How do you know?" She asked, "How do you know you can simply promise me this?".

"Because life with you is easy. I have never known easy before this. Even in the worst scenario, somehow I look at you and I am calm. Violet.. you keep me grounded when my head begins to soar. That is not something I am willing to let go. I will fight for you, not your father, not Niran, not even for this kingdom. I am fighting for you because every day we separate is an eternity of emptiness in my heart and I refuse to feel that way ever again.". He declared.

A Violet Night

She climbed up on top of him kissing him again and wrapping her legs around him. "I know one thing for sure." He said. She looked at him confused. "I will miss the taste of you." He said hungrily flipping her back on her back. "I love you." She whispered, "I love you more." He said smiling down at her. "Most." She said pulling his body down by hers "Forever." He said kissing her lips before entering her body. "Always." She moaned. "Always my princess, always." He said kissing her against her neck.

His breath was hot against her skin, sending shivers through her body. "You are my special girl." He whispered to her as she arched her back for him.

A Violet Night

<u>Chapter 22.)</u>

They jumped at the sound of the door handle jiggle, followed by a knock. "Violet it has time to start getting ready." She heard Elda say through the cracked door. "Just a little longer." She shouted back at her. Rory took both of his hands off of her chest. She pulled them back onto her body. He held her hips. Violet waved her body up and down on his lap. He moaned finishing inside of her. She threw her head back as Rory brought his fingers to her throat. Pulsating and still inside her he pulled her back to his body. Kissing her lips and forehead. "Violet it's time for me to leave.. They are probably out looking for me by now.".

She looked at him as the tears once more filled her eyes. She didn't want him to leave her. "Shhh." He whispered clinging her to his chest "No more tears my dear. I will always come back to you in one way or another... We always kind of knew this would happen one day.." He stood up carrying her body and setting her on the edge of the bed. Walking into the other room and returning with her robe. He slid her arms into it and tied it off for her snug and neatly around her waist. Rory kissed her forehead again slowly and soft letting his lips linger "If something happens to me Violet do not be sad. Remember me as I am now, right here in this moment." He said moving her into his embrace one more time. "I love you." She whispered again. "I know." He said smiling kissing her on the lips.

Just as quickly as he had come he had gone, opening the door letting Elda in. She too looked at him with great sadness "I am going to miss you, you menace.". Rory laughed hugging the old women tightly. "Just don't die, okay?" She said shoving him off of her. "I will do my best not to." He said winking at Violet closing the door behind him. She found herself letting out a grin.

"Come child." Elda said with her arms open. Violet ran to her. She had finally run out of tears to cry. Leaving her empty inside once more. Only this time she plunged deeper into the darkness within the depths of herself.

"I would love to tell you everything will be fine, but I cannot tell you something I do not know Violet. Although I do know you are one of the toughest little girls I have ever had the pleasure of raising." Elda said with a smile. "You will get through this my sweet baby.". Violet hugged her; she smelled her hair as she leaned into it. It smelled of vanilla, spices, and cinnamon. It calmed her in ways beyond her expectation. Relaxing her body the way it did when she was younger. "Let us get this shipwreck a float."

She said standing her posture up right looking sternly into her eyes.

The faint trumpets of war filled their ears from a distance. "First." Elda said pointing to the balcony taking her left hand into Violets sweaty right palm. Violet squeezed it hard and walked over watching as the guards marched out of the kingdom. Violets heart sank. She still couldn't believe this was real. Her eyes searched and scanned the rows of men, but she could not find him from her stance.

Lost in her own anxiety and fear she felt a hand on her shoulder. She turned her head to reveal Scarlet. She let out a weak smile and placed her own hand on hers. "Come now child, they have gone." Elda said walking towards the privy, "I'm going to draw you a hot lavender bath, we need to cleanse him out of you before tonight.". Scarlet moved her hand around Violets shoulders walking her into the room to sit in her chair. She pulled her head to her chest as she sat.

Violet had no words to speak. Her heart ached longing to be held in Rory's tender arms once more. She stumbled numbly to Elda and Scarlets motions helping her into the tub of hot water. It simmered around her body turning her skin bright red, but she had gone numb to the tingling and burning sensation.

In a blue glass bottle Elda poured a mixture of lavender, and chamomile oil into the water. She swirled it with her hand leaning over the tub pouring it on Violets body as Scarlet pulled her back by her shoulders to relax. Elda pulled out a lemon from her pocket, she hummed to herself as she pulled it apart with her fingers using her palms to gently squeeze the juice into the water.

Violet looked into the water watching the cloudy juice and seeds from the lemon mix with the thick oils and shriveled flowers glistening in the light. Elda continued her work pouring in thick frothy milk mixture with raw honey she had been boiling. "Now we let it do its job to rejuvenate your body." she said running her fingers through Violets soaking wet hair still humming to her softly. She kissed her on the back of the head. "Go put the towels and clean robe by the fire for warmth." She told Scarlet pointing with her eyes across the room. "Yes ma'am." She said doing as she was told to retrieve the items.

After a long while of soaking, shaving, and washing her with a bar of goats milk and oat soap. They stood her up out of the tub patting her body dry and rubbing lotion on her skin. They slipped her arms into her robe and walked her to her bed. Elda sat beside her on the edge brushing her long hair out for her. Scarlet walked to the balcony pulling the doors shut and latching them at the top and bottom.

They carefully tucked her body in bed underneath the sheets and heavy covers. "I'll stay with her." Scarlet whispered to Elda as she crawled on top of the bed. Arrow paced around the floor before jumping up next to Violet laying her head at the foot of the bed. Elda nodded "I will be back after you rest, there is still much to be done today.". Violet's eyes began to feel heavy as she succumb to her rest. She dreamt of nothing. Total abyss.

"It is time." Elda's voice rang out as she reopened to balcony doors pouring in tons of evening light bouncing off every surface in the room. Violet fluttered opened her eyes still praying it was all just a bad dream. She saw Harriet carry in the freshly sewn together wedding dress and hung it in front of the vanity where the incrusted jewels and beading caught the sun in the most perfect way.

They evening events began to blur together while they raced together to try and make Violet look whole. Fastening the lace on the long sleeve white lace dress Violet couldn't help but hear all on the giggly chamber maids in her ear go on about how '*lucky*' she was.

Harriet even with a silent scowl on her face and no words to say to her did her hair braided in a bun with little white flowers coming out of it. Her baby hairs dangled at the edges of her hair line elegantly.

Finally Elda placed the vail on top center back of her head. "Beautiful." She whispered with a halfhearted smile "I know this isn't what you envisioned, but you really are a beautiful bride Vi." Harriet said looking her over once more.

Violet looked at her through the long mirror. A man came in the room and whispered into Elda's ear. She looked uneasy as she told Violet it was time to go. They ushered her to the chapel.

The captain stood at the doors his posture heavy and concerned. "Are you ready?" He asked. "My father?" She asked not wanting to let go of Elda's arm "He is inside already… He.. -Uh could barely walk down here on his own today.". She nodded. "Violet?" Harriet said from behind her handing her a white rose bouquet lined gold dipped lilies. Violet looked at her emptily as she placed it in her hands. At a loss for words she hugged her cousin swiftly. Violet did not hug her back. "I'll see you inside." She released her grip and slipped through the doors.

The captain held out his arm. She took it in her own. "It is not to late." He whispered into her ear. Violet looked up at him opening her mouth, but no words followed her quickly gathering thoughts.

Instrumentals started to play from within. The doors of the chapel opened the room was overflowing with people and huge bouquets of white and gold flowers. Sage cloth wrapped and lined the pews and floors. All were turning their heads to look at her.

Violet began to walk down the aisle slowly dragging her feet. She wanted to be sick. She gripped his arm tighter. He looked down at her worried and squeezed her arm back trying to calm her.

She met Nirans gaze. His eyes where a black hole of nothingness beaming into her soul. The captain let go of her reluctantly giving her hands over to Nirans. He gripped them softly overlapping with her bouquet. She made eye contact with Scarlet standing in the back corner her eyes screamed *"We can still run!"*.

Violets empty eyes turned to face Niran once more. He flashed his white teeth at her "How lucky are you." He stated. Violet tightened her grip on her bouquet. There it was again *"How lucky am I?"* Harriet with heavy hands took her bouquet from her and regained her place at her side.

Violet looked into the audience of faces most of whom she could not even name. Her Mother and Father sitting next to each other in the front. Her father barley clinging to life leaning onto her mother, and beside him the captain who had taken the empty seat next to him to balance his leaning.

Violet wanted to scream and race out of the room. She wanted to run. Run as fast and as far as she could possibly go until her legs gave out from beneath her. Even then that would not be far enough away from here.

The vows where said. Her concentration was broken with the dreaded "Niran you may kiss your bride.". Violets stomach dropped as he leaned in he grabbed the back of her head forcefully with the palm of his hand and kissed her. She pulled back as he hyped up the crowd of people now standing and clapping their hands loudly. Women were crying, and men were chanting. He thrust their hands interlocked up into the air popping Violets shoulder in the process. He walked her out of the chapel hand in hand, leading the packed mass hoard out behind them. His hand was sweaty she looked up at his side profile studying him.

His smile opened bearing his teeth as he noticed her watching him. He leaned down to her ear "Are you watching me little mouse?". She looked ahead still feeling his stare. He let out a small nervous laugh.

They entered the ballroom together for the feast of all feasts to take place. After a small coronation and a renouncing of the late king and queens titles they took their place at the head table where her parents would usually be placed.

Meals and desserts began to be passed around the large table. She had no appetite and scooted the food around on her plate with her silverware. She watched the dancers dance and whirl around the room with their bright sheer clothing. The band began to play their instruments loudly in an upbeat motion.

She watched as her father waved weakly at her from the back of the room before her mother and a couple other people helped him leave. Every "Congratulations" hit her like a knife being twisted in her chest being constantly pulled out and replaced in her heart with one sharper then the last. "She is just saving her voice for me." Niran joked to two men and their wives as they left the table with a laugh.

"I know this is all foreign to you, but you will have to start putting on a better face for your company Violet." He whispered to her through a smile. He put one of her small lose strands of hair behind her ear. She looked at him angrily. He licked his lip getting lost in thought.

A Violet Night

Chapter 23.)

"Come." Niran said to Violet. She did as she was told and followed him hesitantly leaving the ball room to their new chambers. Her hands were shaking. She knew what was lying ahead for her, and she wasn't ready. *I could fight back* she thought to herself. This time she would be ready for him. In an instant he motioned towards the bed. Violet sat her heart pounding in the worst way.

He laughed with a trace of ambiance in his tone pouring himself another glass of whiskey from the table in the center of the room. He walked over to the already roaring fireplace taking a drink looking her over slowly.

A Violet Night

"Relax. I will have my way with you, but not tonight." He paused swirling his cup in his fingers before downing another sip. Violet took a breath of relief and felt her body untense itself.

"No. Tonight I have other arrangements." He said looking back at her grinning. A gush of air hit Violet when the doors to the side room opened. A tall woman with a cloak covering her face walked to Niran clinging onto his side embrace. She removed her hood. Violet's gasped.

Visha smiled bitterly at Violet and finished off his cup. She licked her lips looking at Niran full of lust with her siren eyes. He smiled at her aggressively and then back at Violet. He came to her cupping her chin with his thumb wiped her bottom lip pressing hard against her teeth.

Violet felt her body begin to tense up again. Everything began to piece together in her mind... It all finally made sense.

A Violet Night

Niran Pulled Visha closer to him. She kissed him. He looked back at Violet, "I trust you two need no introduction then?". Visha opened her mouth playfully swirling her tongue on the inside of her cheek exposing her very large two front teeth.

Violet felt her mouth gape open a bit. "Close your mouth whore." Visha spat, her words cutting like razors in the thick air. "Ah…. You thought him going war was a coincidence?" He laughed. "No. No, no my dear. You can't be that ignorant, can you?... or maybe you can be?".

Violet opened her mouth farther to speak but no words followed. "You need not speak." He smiled at her devilishly "You may go." He said kissing Visha again.

Violet couldn't move. "Well go on!" He shouted at her "I wish to fuck her in peace!". She smiled dropping her cloak standing there naked with her small breast, and wide hips. Violet realized why Rory could have taken an interest in her. She felt the anger fill her body.

Violet stood and made her way to the door. "Wait." Visha stopped "Make her watch.". Niran almost spit whiskey out of his nose. Choking. looking at her with wide eyes for a moment he said "I knew I liked you. Come. Sit." He said placing a chair directly in front of the bed patting the light pink cushion, he bite his bottom lip at Violet.

Against everything in her body she sat in the chair. They both climbed on the bed. Violet looked at her hands in her lap. "Eyes up here." He said as he spit on himself and entering her from behind. Her face only inches from Violets she could feel her hot breath on her while she moaned "This is how *he* used to fuck me too." She said with a smile.

She let her eyes soon glair past Visha. She watched as her body jiggled with every powerful thrust he threw at her. It went on for a very long time, or so it felt to her. When they finished Visha smiled at Violet hungrily. Violet stared through her smile. Standing up still naked twirling Violets hair in her hand as her bare breast danced in her face.

"Out there you maybe my queen. But in these walls she owns more than you ever will." He watched the two women together. "Now leave before I make you two do things to each other." He said waving Violet on dismissively.

Violet opened the doors to her chambers, and for a second she was fine. She was lost in her memories from the night before. Arrow barked from the bed wagging her tail profusely. She laid down by the dog letting her cuddle up next to her. She pat her on the head letting her hand linger.

Turning and laying on her stomach burying her face in the pillow. She heard something crumble under the pillow. She reached her hand underneath it and pulled out a piece of tea colored paper. She sat up bringing the paper closer to the lit candles so she could read the scribbles inside.

"I lay here. I lay here in the dark alone in my bed, with one million things on my mind. That is one million things I cannot change. One million things I cannot touch, see, or even feel and with knowing all of that it still traps me in an imprisonment of clad iron bars. With chains so heavy I cannot move. I cannot feel. I cannot even let out a breath. It is like I am drowning, as all of my worries, fears, all of the opinions of irrelevant people fill my lungs like cold sharp water. I gasp for air which is you. Even though some days that in itself is not enough. I am drowning. Drowning in one million things we call life, and Violet you are my breath of air that takes me away from these chains. And for that I can't thank you enough, I love you more then you will ever begin to understand. -Ri."

A Violet Night

Violet smiled. A tear fell onto the note. "I love you most." She whispered amongst herself. "Is this spot taken?" Scarlet said sliding into bed next to her. She hadn't even heard her enter the room. She shook her head no "I thought you could use some company after such a ling day.". "Thank you." Violet said weakly recomposing herself and folding the note over again in her hands.

"I took your dog out for a while, I hope that was okay?" Scarlet said trying to come up with something more to say. Violet climbed off her bed and put the note inside of a red book on the top shelf before coming back to lie down. She blew out the candle next to the bed and went to sleep still in her dress.

A Violet Night

Chapter 24.)

Violet looked at her father's shallow breaths few in between and crossed her arms "So you say she took most of her belongings?". "Yes my Queen. Everything is accounted for except some articles of clothing, her jewelry, a couple bags of currency and the tapestry painting of you and your sister." Conn said looking at the torn apart closet "There is no sign of foul play present.".

"Should we rally the search parties?" Another man asked. Violet shook her head at him "No... Even a fool can see she left of her own free will. If she wishes to return she will.". "But your majesty-" he began.

"Are you deaf? She said let it be. We mustn't waist our time on those who wish not to be found." Niran chimed in wrapping his arm around her waist.

Violet glanced at him with her eyes and took a small step to try and sperate them. He tightened his grip on her pulling Violet closer. "I am sorry my King." the man said bowing in hopes of forgiveness. "I am sure you are…You may go now." Niran said onto them "We wish to be alone in such trying times.".

With the sound of the door closing Violet tore his arm off of her. He rolled his eyes at her. "I suppose I am supposed to thank you." She said grateful he had cleared the room. Since the time she had awoken she had been bombarded with nonstop issues.

"I felt like you could use the time." He said sitting in a chair at the head of her fathers bed. She scoffed "Alone? Wouldn't that mean for you to leave as well?". He ignored her questioning. "You should spend this time with him Violet. There isn't much left." He said stretching his back in the chair while extending his long legs. "Come have a seat." He said patting his lap twice with an eager grin.

Violet looked at him disgusted and sat at the end of the bed just close enough to hold her father's hand. "Suit yourself my darling dear. One day you will beg me to sit here, and I will make you squirm for it." He said widening his grin.

"Do you really think she would just up and leave?" She changed the subject trying to ignore his perversion. "Oh I know she did." He said matter of factly. She looked at him full of questions. "I watched her leave before the morning sun with a horse and a pack on her back." He said blankly licking his two fingers from bottom to top bringing his gaze back to her to put out the candle beside him. She continued staring him over. He raised his eyebrows shaking his head slightly.

"I couldn't sleep last night.." he said looking at her father "I came down to their chambers a couple times last night to check on him. The last time is when I saw her out the window.".

The doctor entered the room with his mask and floor length coat. "Come, let him do his work." Niran said offering to help Violet stand. She ignored his hand and began to walk past him and the doctor with his silver tray of elixirs and instruments.

"Alright. I'll see you later.. My *Queen.*" He said loudly as she walked down the hall. She didn't want to look back at him.

"Walk with me." Conn said coming up beside her walking with his hands tucked neatly behind his back. "He is safe. For now at least." He said quietly to her. "Thank

you." She said giving herself some peace of mind.

"I leave in a little while to be overseer of the camp

and another nearby so I may keep a close eye on my

nephew.." he stopped to look at her "I worry what will

happen to you when I leave." He said tenderly. "You

mustn't worry about me!" She said with a smile placing her

hand on his shoulder. "No of course not." He said smiling

"You know.. watching you grow up has been one of the

highlights of my life." He said, "It has been an honor to

serve your family.". "Why do you say this with such tone?"

she asked. "My dear girl, there is not enough time in this

life for unsaid words that we wish we could have spoken."

He replied. She reach up and hugged him "Please return

him to me." She whispered. He nodded his head "I will do

my best.".

Conn escorted Violet to the dining hall where she

ate and returned to her chambers with Scarlet and Arrow at

her side. She began parting Scarlets hair into multiple parts between her fingers to braid when Harriet walked in. She crossed her arms and paced around the room "I leave tomorrow." She said sincere worry on her tongue. The room stayed silent.

"I know it is not your choice Violet, but you need to except what is best." She said shifting her frustration onto her cousin. Violet stopped braiding and looked up. *"What's best?"* she thought to herself. She scoffed shaking her head angrily and continued to twist the hair in her fingers pulling just a little harder.

"Can't you stay?" Scarlet asked feeling the tension rising in the room. Harriet watched Violet overly concentrate on her braiding, "No.. My father's absence being in the war front is taking a toll on my mother. She needs my help keeping things in order.".

A Violet Night

"Then you should go. Why wait until tomorrow when you could leave tonight?" Violet said sternly. "You do not have to act like this, you know?" Harriet said taken back. "Act like what Harriet?" She said back looking at her daringly. "Like a brat Violet. You are being childish. So what you miss rag boy. So what you *'loved'* him. You have a new role here. One any women would die to have the chance at! So get over yourself and your pitiful pride." She yelled gripping her dress.

Filled with rage Violet calmly pointed at the door "So let them come and die for it then, and let you leave now.". "Like I said, childish Violet." She staggered in the doorway "When you are ready to be an adult, I will be ready to listen." She said quietly closing the door behind her.

Violet tied off Scarlets two connecting braids with a ribbon. "Who does she think she is anyways?" She said crossing her arms angrily. Scarlet pushed her fingers on her tight scalp pulling the tight hairs looser. "I do not want to be involved, but I think you are being a bit hard on her." Scarlet said. Violet took a deep breath in looking at the door.

Another knock at the door. "Go away Harriet!" Violet shouted. A small slender maid walks in and bowed in her presence "Your grace. The king has requested your presence immediately.". "No." she said looking up briefly. "I-I'm sorry my Queen but he said if you were to say no that Harriet may have an *accident* on her travels home..".

Violet looked up at her and took a long moment to get off of the bed and follow her to his chambers. She opened the door without knocking.

Niran was straddling the chair from last night sitting backward with his arms crossed over the top resting his head firmly on them. Violet jumped at the sound of the door closing behind her

A Violet Night

"Disrobe." He said watching her. Violet stood there stunned. "Do not make me say it twice." He said harshly. She took off her clothes slowly and hesitantly covering herself with her hands. He waved his hand in a spinning motion. Turning in a circle she looked only at the floor shamefully. "Get on the bed." He demanded now standing unfastening his belt and pants.

She stopped in front of the bed. He shoved her down by the back of her neck so that she was leaning over it. He spanked her on the ass Violet flinched. "It is almost like you know how much your fear turns me on." He said grabbing a fist full of her hair close to the scalp pulling her head back.

"But first a drink." He whispered grabbing the wine bottle next to him. With her hair still in his hand and her head still tilted back he began to flood it into her gaping mouth. "Open wide for me my Queen." He wrapped his arm around to grab her throat and jaw making her open her mouth farther.

It overflowed while she choked it down. Violet could feel the wine pour down her bare chest and onto the bed. The red wine trickled down his white sleeve while he brought the bottle to his own lips "What am I doing?" He chuckled throwing the bottle across the room. She flinched again hearing it explode on the wall. "There is something about you Violet that gets me flustered inside." He excitedly exclaimed.

He pulled her back to him aggressively, so her back was pulled against his chest. She took a deep breath in as he loosened his grip on her throat letting his hand lower to the base of her neckline. Niran swept her hair to the side gently and slowly as he leaned in to lick the sticky wine from her neck all the way to the base of her ear. She shivered. She felt his lips form into a smile against her skin. "You have kept this from me for far too long." He whispered deeply pinning her arms behind her back holding them both at the wrist with one of his hands.

In a swift instant then shoving her face down into the bed. "Climb." He demanded letting go of her with his palm and her hands with the other. She climbed up on top of the bed still on all fours. She heard the jingling sound of his pants hit the floor beneath the bed. She tried to prepare herself as she felt his body weight shift the bed beneath them and his wine stained shirt flew in front of her landing on a pillow.

He spread her open savoring a moment for himself to taste her and spit inside of her. She felt him grab at her flesh in his hands while he rubbed up her spine pressing down at her waist. She let out a small gasp as he painfully entered her. "It's okay. I know you like it." He said forcing his way in harder and faster. She let out a small sound trying her best to look ahead. He tightened his grip on her hips. She felt her face begin to well up with tears "*Not here.*" She thought to herself sucking them back up. She

felt him pulsate inside her while he let out a loud grunting

sound. Niran grabbing the headboard above them pushing

himself deeper inside of her.

He pulled himself out of her one tear fell down her

cheek. Violet felt what he left gush out of her with every

slight movement. She remained on all fours. She jumped

slightly feeling Nirans thumb brush against her opening. "I

can finally say I've had you now." He said his voice low

and graveled. "Face me." He demanded. She turned around

slowly. He pulled her face up to his level by her jaw. He

looked down over her bare body.

He pinched with his fingers to open her mouth, and

with his thumb he rubbed himself on her tongue. Violet

gagged on the inside trying to remain silent. He looked at

her possessively and smiled biting his lip. He let her go

laying back to relax. Violet covered herself up with the

blanket quickly.

A Violet Night

He laughed putting his hands behind his head trying to catch his breath. "Oh, uhm your father died earlier this evening also. I told them I would deliver the news to you personally." He said emotionless.

Violet pulled her knees to her chest looking at the flames across the room crackle. "When will you speak to me?". "I will speak only when you are dead." She said muffled into the blanket. "There's my feisty girl." He said reaching over and brushing her cheek with the outside of his hand. She pushed it away.

"May I go now?" She said looking into the fire now grasping at the bedding she wrapped around her naked body. "What fun would that be?" He said tugging at her side of the bedding.

She continued to look off. He sighed heavily, "I fucking tried to be nice to you you cunt.". Grabbing her by the hair again he pulled her face up to his. She could smell the wine and herself on his lips. With his other hand he pinched one of her cheeks with his index finger and thumb.

He let go of her hair and stroked her face once more. She shoved his hand away. "You can find a way to be happy in this new life, or you can be miserable." He said to her. Violet spit in his face. He grinned wiping it off of himself. He looked the saliva over in his hand and smiled slapping her across the face just hard enough to make her sting. Violet looked up at him. She could taste the blood in her mouth pooling. "I'd do it again." She whispered. "I know you will." He said with a laugh "And I yearn for you to do it again Violet.".

He grabbed her by the arm and squeezed hard. "That is why every day from now on will be amazing with you. Darling you may come out now." He threw her to the floor coldly as Visha walked out of the closet. "I like to watch and be watched." She said with a grin prancing over to the fire prodding it with the fire poker until it grew red hot.

"You may have your fun now darling she has bored me." He said sitting up on the side of the bed now putting his pants back on. "With pleasure my King." She said smiling walking to Violet. "Visha please." Violet whimpered looking up at her. "On your knees." She said looking at the red hot metal in her hands Violet opened her mouth to speak "I said on your knees!" She yelled loudly. Violet did so hesitantly.

With the burning hot poker she pressed it against Violets skin just below both of her collar bones. Violet hissed in pain. She felt her flesh begin to melt against the iron. She heard it sizzle when it left her skin pulling it as it did so. "Now you will always have a reminder of the one who took everything from you." She said to her. "Now get out of here.".

A Violet Night

Niran looked at Visha with a look of almost sadness for second before nodding to Violet to leave. He handed over her dress calmly. She ripped it out of his hands. Nirans energy felt somehow different now. She scrambled to put the dress back on, and out the door she flew.

A Violet Night

Chapter 25.)

"You didn't have to burn her. People will start to question me if they notice marks on her body I cannot explain.". Niran said with a stern worry in his voice. Visha laughed "Do you pity her? Or did you not just strike her in the face?". He took a moment to recompose himself.

He snatched her by the throat "Do not ever question me." He said throwing her lanky body to the ground. She looked up at him scornfully. "Do not ever forget your place here Visha. You are nothing without me. Just like you are nothing with me. That ground you lay on means more to me than your life ever will. Now leave at once, before I too use the fire in ways your mind can not even begin to digest.". She hesitantly started the get up with a hint of fear across her face. He knocked her back down with the heal of his boot "Crawl. Like the worthlessness you are.". She looked up at him as his eyes widened, and she began to crawl to the door on all fours.

He took a deep inhale putting his two hands above his head. He looked around the room at the mess he had created. "Why am I like this?" He asked out loud. His veins grew hot with rage. "What is wrong with me!" He shouted grabbing one of the other chairs and throwing it across the room watching the legs of it break off as it smashed against the wall. He looked around the room taking in deep breaths and counting to try and calm himself.

He picked up his mess of glass, and the broken chair. Wiping up the spills with his white shirt off the bed.

A Violet Night

He tossed the shirt into the fire watching it crackle and pop as he tossed parts of the broken chair on top.

"My King your meeting has already begun." A guard said opening the door. "So it has." He said slipping into a navy blue silk shirt.

Meeting after royal meeting that night he placed his head on his cool pillow. He quickly fell asleep stretched out in his enormous bed alone. He stretched his hand out to the extra pillow beside him imagining and reminiscing how it felt to lay next to Ann. He missed her so much.

He began to think of the day and how he had treated Violet. An overwhelming feeling of guilt passed through his stomach. *"She didn't deserve that."* He thought to himself while he closed his eyes *"Ann would never have let me act in such a way."*.

"Mother have you seen Ann?" He cheerfully said grabbing at his undone cufflink. He smiled approaching her. A short dark headed woman turned around with her stone-cold green eyes "Oh yes, I have seen her today.". "And where may your future daughter in law be at on this fine beautiful morning?" He said still smiling at the thought of his bride to be.

"At the bottom of the creek one may hope." She said turning and walking away. Niran looked at his mother "Out of all the disgusting things you say why do you insist on speaking of her in this way? She is the perfect woman, kind, gentle, soft, and warm.". His mother cackled at him "You mean spineless, feeble, and WEAK! You are a strong brilliant man Niran. You should not waist your precious time on an ideal of 'family' with such an of imbecilic nature.".

He shook his head at her violently. "Do not talk to me about family or love when you do not know the first thing about loving someone or putting their needs before your own.". "You're right Niran. I do not know anything about love do I?" She paused straightening the ruffles in her black dress. She leaned into her sons face, ruffling his combed over hair "That is why Ann is in the bottom of the creek." She leaned away from him to watch the terror in his eyes as he searched her face for a break. She smiled at him and began to turn away from him. "You're lying!" He screamed. His heart dropped out of his chest. She chuckled to herself pointing out the pillared windows "There might still be time to save her. That is if my men haven't already gotten to her first.".

He ran. He ran the fastest he had ever before as thousand thoughts crossed over into his mind. He tripped down the large front staircase scrambling to his feet, through the front yard, down the large grassy hill, and down to the muddy creek bed. Tumbling on the large rocks he struggled to get back to his feet as they then continuously sank beneath his weight in the muck.

A Violet Night

He could see something yellow in the distance laying on the shore. He began to run faster. "NO. NO. NO!" He screamed frantically at the top of his lungs, tears filling his eyes and blurring his vision. He fell to his knees flipping over the cold limp body of the love of his life. He screamed again to the heavens above praying they would hear his cries.

Her lips where blue. She had been down here a while. Her beautiful eyes open staring up lifelessly towards the sky. He brushed her hair out of her face kissing her forehead and lips pulling her in closer to his body. He sobbed until his head began to throb with his own heartbeat. He moved his hand from behind her head to close her eyes. "I will see you again my sunshine." He whispered in her ear rocking her lifeless body in his arms. His tears streamed down his face dripping in a pitter-patter onto her body. He brought her head to his praying she would open her eyes or call out his name.

A Violet Night

"Pathetic!" His mother said looking at him lacking empathy. He looked up at her his lips trembling "How could you! I loved her mother!" his tears began to fall again harder with anger. She kneeled down to her sons eye level "Love is for the weak my son. Power triumphs everything in this life. The sooner you know this the less it will hurt." She stood back up and motioned to the man next to her "Clean up your mess.". He nodded his head "Yes ma'am." he began to approach them. "Do not come near us." Niran said with his eyes closed. He stood up with Ann's body in his arms. Her head fell onto his chest. "I will send word of the accident at once to her family." His mother said still walking away.

Niran creaked open the door to his mother's chambers while she slept. He looked at her resting body watching her chest rise and fall. His fist began to shake as his sides. "She should be breathing this sweet air not you.". He said grabbing a pillow from the end of her bed. He shoved the pillow over her face. Waking up out of her sleep she began to scream muffled into the pillow. Panicking she wailed her arms around desperately trying to pull it off. She scratched at his hands he jumped on top of her body forcing the pillow farther into her face. Her feet began to flare.

He leaned down and lightly gave way with the pillow. "Niran!" she screamed gasping terrified. "Love is for the weak." He said as he began to suffocate her again.

She continued to try and fight him off until.. nothing. Her hands dropped beside her. He waited a few moments to make sure she was dead, and then slumped his exhausted body to the floor with the pillow still in one hand. A tear fell from his face. He wiped it away. Standing up he fixed her body in the bed, placing the pillow back at the end like nothing had happened. He slipped back out of the door. Looking once more at her lifeless corpse.

A Violet Night

Niran awoke drenched in sweat sitting up as fast as he could. His heart racing from his dream of the past. He calmed himself down looking around the room.. He grinned to himself with an uneasy laugh, "Love is for the weak.". He looked to his right it was still dark outside the cool breeze sweep across his skin. He leaned down picking up the covers he had kicked off from the floor.

A Violet Night

<u>Chapter 26.)</u>

Violet erupted from underneath the steaming, simmering water. Her gasp for air became labored breathing as she began to sob amongst herself. She hyperventilated stuttering her breath. Violet took her bathing brush and ferociously scrubbed herself over and over until her body stung.

"Violet I think you should get out now.. You have been in here long enough to turn into a fish." Scarlet joked uneasily from the other side of the locked door. Violet staired emptily at the glowing embers of the fireplace. The room was almost as dark as the night sky outside. "Okay..

Well I am not leaving until I know you are okay." Scarlett muttered quietly.

Violet slowed her scrubbing looking at her forearm. She dropped the brush into the water hearing it clank against the bottom of the tub. She grasp her arm in her hand pulling it to her chest. She leaned back onto the tubs inclined edging.

She was disgusted at herself for not fighting back. "*Never again.*" She thought to herself. Violet stood up and stepped out of the tub leaving behind a trail of wet footprints.

"Finally!" Scarlet exclaimed quickly looking away again embarrassed "I think you forgot some vital clothing choices." She said looking back over "Violet.. Your skin is raw!" She ran up to Violet who was now almost to the door. "Violet come let's get dressed you know not what you are doing." She pulled at her hands to turn around looking at her collar bones and broken patches of flesh on her arms.

"Violet! You are scaring me!" She said cautiously. Violet cracked a smile looking up into Scarlets eyes. Scarlet shivered glancing away for a second. "You are not the one who should fear me." She ripped her hands away from her. Scarlet placed her hand on the door to stop it from opening. "Violet.. You are indecent.." She said pushing the cracked door closed. Violet looked at her emotionless "I am just as I was the day I came into this hellish world. Now move. Let do what I have to do.". "And what is it that you have to do?" Scarlet said loosening her grip on the door to cross her arms. "I am going to kill him." Violet said walking out into the hall.

Scarlet uncrossed her arms rushing to get in front of Violet who effortlessly pushed her to the side "You have not thought this through enough. Plans sought out in anger never succeed Vi.". Scarlet awkwardly made eye contact with a guard as the passed by in the hall. Violets fists were balled at her waist. Her knuckles were turning white as they approached Nirans quarters. Scarlet through herself in front of Violet "Violet STOP." She whispered frantically searching for any reasoning in her eyes grabbing her shoulders "I am going to find Elda!". "Tell her the king is dead." Violet said knocking her hands off one by one. Without any hesitation she creaked open the door and walked inside. Scarlett took off down the hall, her small heels clicking ferociously.

Niran sleepily looked up from his bed. After taking a second to come to reality he sat up rubbing his eyes childlike. Violets wet her dangled around her face slapping her in the back. She slowly approached the bed. "Come back for seconds now did we?" He asked intrigued looking her over. Violet climbed up on top of his chest straddling him between her thighs. He wrapped his arms around her bottom half gripping it tightly. She leaned over him and grabbed the two long braided ties holding the bed curtains open.

"Violet-" He started. "Shut up!" She roared. He pulled his head back awestruck. His eyes grew huge. "Are you raising your voice at your king?" He asked rubbing up her body's curves. "Lay back." She demanded pinning his hands down on each side of his head. He opened his mouth twisting his tongue around before biting his lip. She tied one of his hands tightly to the bed frame. "What is this?" He asked smiling still trying to touch her body with his free hand. Violet looked into his eyes scornfully as she finished tying his second hand "I said SHUT UP!".

She said turning around gracefully still straddling his chest. She slowly began to lean forward arching her back upwards exposing all of herself to him. "You just want to be fucked don't you." He moaned from his lips praying to touch her. She flipped her hair back over her shoulders as she slowly rubbed up his legs bringing herself back around to his face. She went in as if she was going to kiss him breathing into his mouth she whispered, "You are going to taste what it is like to come face to face with death himself." He smiled at her ready for anything she wanted to do to him.

"May he bring you no mercy." Violet climbed over his face until she could feel his hot deep breathing down below. "Sit." He begged "Let your king feast!". Violet smiled teasing him dropping herself on him and then back off. "Let me taste you!" He shouted. "As you wish." She said sitting on his face. Violet smiled to herself as she swirled her hips around. She could feel his tongue moving around and inside her rapidly. She watched his legs become frantic and his breathing become fast. Her skin vibrated as he tried to talk from under her body. She smiled bearing her weight onto his face even more.

She noticed something moving from the corner of her eye. She looked up "He cannot breathe!" Visha exclaimed rushing into the room. She shoved Violet off of

him. She looked at him worried. His face dripping wet from

Violet. "More! I did not say I was finished!" He said trying

to catch his breath "How dare you interrupt my meal." He

said to Visha angrily. Visha darted her eyes to each of them

"Well, continue." She said tossing her hand in the air.

Violet looked around "No. I think we are done here.". "I

say when we are finished." Niran said looking at only her.

Violet softened her brow.

"I think I will stay." Visha announced. Violet

shrugged standing up bumping her in the process. "Suit

yourself, he is all yours." Violet paused slipping into

Nirans shirt from the end of the bed. It fluttered down just

above her knees. She effortlessly pulled her damp hair out

of the collar stretching her hands above her head elongating

her body. She made eye contact with Niran who was

pulling to sit up on his elbows. "I suppose death has not

claimed you on this day." She walked to the door slowly knowing all eyes were on her.

"I didn't say you could excuse yourself." He said smiling to her. Violet stopped at the door frame looking into the long dark hallway before disappearing. "Come back and untie me!" He shouted angrily. "I can pick up where she left off." Visha said tracing her hand on his chest. He looked to her disgusted. "Untie me." He gritted through his teeth. She untied his right hand "We can still enjoy what was for shadowed upon us." She said kissing his neck. He took a deep breath in while pulling her hair away from his body "Once again you have ruined everything. Why would I ever be surprised that is what you are best at.". She pulled at his hand to let go.

He let her go with a shove of her head. "Now finish untying me.". "Untie yourself!" She said bitterly speeding out of the room. He rolled his eyes annoyed sitting the rest of the way up he undid his other hand. Rubbing both of his rope burned wrist together he looked into the hall hoping Violet would return.

He looked to the window the skyline was turning pink and orange. The birds were singing their songs to the sun.

A Violet Night

Chapter 27.)

"Which one?" Scarlet asked confused from inside

the pantry. She grabbed two jars of thickened liquid lifting

them to the light to see the contents. "The honey dear.

Wrong shelf." Elda said unlacing white clovers from her

knapsack she took them to the fire dumping them all into a

pot of boiling water along with carefully diced ginger. She

took out her wooden spoon. Beginning to stir the liquid

round and around.

Scarlet set the jar down carefully with two hands

"And we are sure she is? I mean maybe she is just not

hungry. After all she has been through a lot these past

couple months.". "She has not bled in nearly four full moons now." Elda said putting a lid over the simmering clovers. "Stress!" Scarlet said reassuring herself. Elda shook her head "Do not be so naïve. She is with child.". "Yeah.. Well that would explain why she has been spewing everything lately." Scarlet said leaning her torso over the countertop "Poor girl can't even hold down water.".

"What does this help with again?" Scarlet asked smelling the wet spoon. Elda snatched it out of her hand raising her eyebrow at her. "Do you even listen when I try and teach you these things? The clovers in this tea will help with her body aches from her bones stretching below. While the ginger will help her keep it all down. Some days I believe those holes on the sides of your head are solely for decoration." She smiled at her jokingly while she strained out the clover and ginger placing it into another jar. "Why not just throw them out?" Scarlet asked watching carefully and curiously. "Everything has more than one purpose my dear.. It is merely a matter of what you do with it." She said in a serious tone drizzling the honey inside the pot mixing it. She leaned in to smell the steam. She carefully ladled 4 swoops into a drinking mug setting it on a serving tray where she had placed some crackers. "Now go to her." She said handing it off to Scarlett.

She grabbed the towel hanging off of her apron and began to wipe down the splattered tea from jarring the leftovers. The sound of soft heels clicking into the kitchen filled her ears. Elda turned around with a smile "What did you forget now?".

Visha sniffled rubbing a tear from her cheek. Elda looked at her confused "Can I get you something? Perhaps a glass of water or a snack to hold you over until dinner?". Visha shook her head recollecting her composure "I was told you are the one to seek for.. uhm.. special remedies...". Elda stood up straighter "Depends.". "On?" Visha asked desperate. "What it is you are needing." Elda said walking behind her to close the door to the hallway. "I need to get rid of a problem.." She said stepping out of Elda's way. "Problem..? How big of a problem?" She said looking at her bruised up upper arms. Visha pulled her shawl over her arms "A baby…". She looked quickly at the wall.

"NOW YOU LISTEN HERE!" She said loudly grabbing her spoon from the countertop to point in her face "I will not give you anything to end her pregnancy.". "Her pregnancy?" Visha asked confused and alarmed. Elda pulled the spoon back "Oh dear me.". "No.. No.. It is for me.." She said looking down at her fingers as her eyes welled up.

Elda cleared her throat choosing her next words carefully "Does he know you are also with child?". She nodded crossing her arms beginning to cry again. Elda's face softened "Is he forcing you to do this? There are other ways around this.". She shook her head again hysterically

"You do not understand… The baby is not his.". "How can you be sure?" Elda asked coming in closer to her. "Niran is always beyond carful. I- I am the one who let my feelings get in the way…" Visha brought her hands to her cheeks "He will kill me if this is not his baby.. Please! You have to help me!". Elda sighed pitying her.

She opened the walk in cabinet climbing the ladder. Elda grabbed dried red raspberry leaf, dried hibiscus, and yarrow. "Here." She said handing the bottles and jars down to Visha. She stepped off the ladder and from the bottom shelf she grabbed nettle and one cinnamon stick along with an empty jar.

She carefully looked Visha over deciding her measurements "How far along?" she asked. "I cannot be sure.. It happened when we visited the war camps.". Elda inhaled sharply "About three moons ago?". Visha nodded timidly. "One stick of cinnamon, two spoons of nettle, two spoons of raspberry, two spoons of yarrow and a half handful of hibiscus." She said combining the dry ingredients. She filled the jar three fourths of the way to the top with boiling water. Visha gulped watching all the particles float to the top. Elda tightened the lid shaking it hard in her hands before placing it in the window. She saw the worry on her face "I will strain it in the morning.. if you decide to go through with this-".

"You do not understand. I do not have a choice." She raised her broken voice. Elda grabbed her frustrated hands "Breathe.. My dear we always have a choice in this life weather it to be from what to wear, what to eat, to run, to stay, to dispose of…" Elda took a moment looking down at Visha's stomach "To keep." She tightened her grip "You cannot leave your own decisions in the hands of such a man. If this is what you decide it will be here waiting for you in the morning.. If you decide to persist I will simply throw out our mixture.".

A Violet Night

"Thank you." Visha said with a faint grin. "Come, drink." Elda said poring a glass of the now cooled down clover tea. Visha took a sip making a slight face "I think I will go lay down if that is okay with you?". "Go on. You have a heavy decision on your chest." Elda said walking her to the door.

After the night was over and the sun had barely rerose over the walls, Elda yawned tying her apron behind her back. Coming into the kitchen for the day "Good morning Ms. Elda." A chipper girl said rummaging through the drawers. Elda nodded at her with a warm smile grabbing the jar from the window giving it another hard shake "Good morning love.". "That woman who is always at the kings side is waiting for you in the dining hall. I tried to offer her something, but she was pretty stuck on seeing you. I understand why of course. No one's meals even begin to compare to yours!" she said beside herself. Elda nodded straining juiced mixture into a drinking glass

"Thank you my dear. The more you watch, and you do the more you will learn. Then before you know it you might be my replacement.". "You think so?" She said grinning ear to ear. "Anything is possible." Elda said leaving the room.

"I have been waiting for you." Visha said coldly. "Good morning to you as well." Elda said setting the glass in front of her. She pulled it back as Visha reached for it with her fingertips "You drink this here in front of me if you are to do this.. for obvious reasons of course.". "*Obvious reasons.*" Visha scoffed. Elda hardened her look "Being ungrateful is not a beautiful look on you my dear child.".

Elda sat at the edge of the table urging her to do the same. "He will kill me and the baby." She said looking around the room nervously. Elda let go of the glass and once more took her hands into her own. "Do you want this?" Elda asked looking at her stomach. Visha nodded "Very much so. I have always wanted to be a mother to his children. I have dreamt of this for years, but to bring a child into this situation.. His beautiful child only to be destroyed is not something I can live with.". "Can you live with yourself if you are the one to destroy this child?" Elda asked, "Life is to precious, and far too short to be under someone's thumb.". Visha took the glass. Her respirations rapidly quickened.

She poured it into a green potted plant behind her chair. "I pray you are right." She said. "Me too." Elda said taking the empty glass from her hands "Otherwise I am going to look like the biggest ass this side of the kingdom. Now go on get some more rest you have bags under your eyes.". "What will I do when the baby is to be born?" She asked nervously "Like I told you last night my dear you are never without choices. We have an infinite amount of ideas to come up with in the coming months. Now go on get some more rest you both need some." Elda pointed at her stomach.

A Violet Night

"Do you have any more of that tea left that you gave me?" She asked shyly. "I have to make some fresh. Someone will bring it to you in your room." Elda said patting her hand.

A Violet Night

<u>Chapter 28.)</u>

Every day came and went into night. The days turned into weeks, and weeks into more months past. The nights came earlier in the day, and the warm air was now chilled. Her mother was still just a breathe in the wind as if she had never lived within the suffocating walls. Not a sign or a trace of her presence lingered in or out. The assumption that she joined the king in the afterlife was the only relief the people could get after the loss of their beloved king.

Violet now noticeably with child rubbed her belly. Although she was unsure who's baby she was even carrying. She unsure how to feel about the arising situation.

A Violet Night

The beatings from Niran had almost completely subsided, but Visha had little to no mercy or at least no mercy for her when Niran was not around.

Visha had not graced anyone with her appearance lately, and Violet was not complaining. It was as if they fed off of each other's energies when they were together two serpents going after her from every direction. On some occasions Violet had even begged for death. She had long since lost her fight within.

"You better bite your tongue next time or I will cut it out baby or no baby inside of you." Niran yelled at Violet. "Fuck off." She said sternly walking towards the stairs. He grabbed her by the neck hard pulling her back to him without squeezing. "Leave her alone." Scarlet said shoving his hand off of her.

He looked at her amused. Violet stood in front of her. "The next time you open your mouth to talk back to your king I will shove my cock down your throat like the little whore you deserve to be.". She smiled bitterly at him squinting her eyes at him. "Oh, you'd like that huh?" he mumbled. Scarlet shook her head "No, I was just wondering how your blood would taste on my tongue when I bite your cock off.". "Remember your place. You get no more chances with me girl." He said walking up the stairs in a jogging motion.

"You alright?" she asked Violet. She nodded her head at her "I'm going to have a rest now. I am not feeling well today." She said placing her hand on top her stomach. "I will walk with you." She said grabbing Violets arm. "Thank you, but I think it is for the better if I go alone in case he is waiting for me. You know how he gets if he sees you in our room." She said with a broken smile. "Are you sure?" Scarlet asked looking up at the top of the staircase. "I am sure he will not harm me." She said with a comforting tone. "I suppose I should go help Elda with lunch then." Scarlet said excusing herself making her way down the hall.

Violet made it to the top of the staircase slowly with one hand on her belly and the other on the cold railing. She smiled catching her breath. Visha walked passed her slowly "That baby you carry will be ours to raise, and I suppose we can raise it with our own." She said smugly rubbing her small but round belly. Violet looked at her shocked she had no clue she was also with child.

Visha smiled stiffly. "It happened when we went to the war camps a couple months back," she paused "You do know if it comes out looking like Rory we will have to kill it. After all it is not like he could raise it from the grave.". Violet looked at her confused. She had to be lying. "Ahh... You really don't know do you?" Visha asked satisfied. "He is dead. Killed in battle by the enemy. We have known of this news for weeks, months even, but telling you now and getting the satisfaction of utter broken heartedness is so fulfilling. The King has been waiting to use this against you the next time you decided to be an arrogant little wench. Such a shame he has grown such a disgusting soft spot for you. Do not get to accustomed to it once that little thing pops out of you things will go back to the way they are rightfully meant to be." She turned and took one step down.

Filled with rage Violet reached to push her. She turned her head back to Violet gripping her dress and the railing to catch her balance "You will regret that, you stupid little bitch.". Visha grabbed Violets arm throwing Violet down the stairs.

Violets heart sank low in her chest. She did her best to protect her belly from the sharp edges of the marble staircase hitting her head off of the statue at the bottom. She looked up to the top again her vision blurry, but she saw what she saw. Niran slit Visha's throat, and her lifeless body toppled down the stairs landing next to her on the ground. Their blood began too pool together. Violets eyes fluttered to stay open. Niran began to race down the stairs to her shouting.

Violet felt a cramp and something wet in between her thighs. She reached down with her fingers bringing them back up covered in thick red blood. Her stomach cramped again, and she cried out for help to him. Niran screamed over her pulling her into his arms standing up frantically.

A guard took her from his arms and carried her to the closest spare room, leaving a trail of dripping dark blood for Niran to follow. Elda and Scarlet followed with rags, towels, and water. "I am not ready!" Violet cried out shaking her head. It was like no one could hear her cries. They ran around the room. Niran crossed one arm and bit the nails on his other hand. "Do you think it is dead?" He asked Elda. She looked at him sad "I am not sure. She has lost a lot of blood, but I do not think you should be in here.".

"Tell me when it's over." He exited the room. "Hey, hey. I'm right here." Scarlet said holding Violets hand and pulling her hair out of her face with the other. Another maiden with a cool rag washed the blood off of Violets head rubbing the knot on the side. Elda reaching in between Violets legs feeling with her fingers making her cramp again and cry loudly "Help me get her up!" Elda shouted pointing around the room wiping her fingers off. Two of the maidens pulled her arms around their shoulders helping her to squat. "My ribs!" Violet howled in pain. "Broken no doubt." Elda said empathetic.

Twisting another wet rag scarlet put it in Violets mouth. "You'll want to bite down on this." She said sweeping her hair out of her face again behind her shoulders. Scarlet traded places with one of the maidens "You can do this Vi." She said trying to assure her. "She has to do this." Elda corrected her laying things out quickly before her.

A Violet Night

She felt a burning sensation and an enormous amount of pressure. Her body knew she had to push. She did her best to squat arm in arm with Scarlet and another maiden screaming through the rag in her mouth. The tears fell from her cheeks and sweat poured from her body. She couldn't hear what everyone was saying over her cries. Her fingertips were numb from gripping their arms. On the fifth push she felt relief and a waterfall of fluids as the baby came into the world.

Thirty seconds passed. It was silent in the room. Violets eyes began to droop. Everything around her was going black and fuzzy. Another large slimy thing exited her body. Her eyes fluttered open and closed before becoming too heavy to reopen them. An overwhelming sensation of peace flowed through her body as she heard her baby's cry fill the air.

Violet felt her body being lifted back onto the bed. There was a ringing in both of her ears and then nothing.

No sounds only darkness. Suddenly she saw him. Rory, his smile made her heart happy. She ran to him her bare feet touching the summer grass. He picked her up hugging her before they both fell to the ground laughing.

Elda watched Violet's even breaths for a moment and then down at the blonde haired little boy covered in his mother's blood in her arms. She smiled rubbing his nose with her thumb before passing him to Scarlet. She placed the placenta into a bowl next to them instructing a guard to cut the cord when it loses its color.

She looked to the floor next to the bed at Visha's limp body that the maids had rushed in. Against her instincts Elda ran to it and with the knife in her left hand she began to cut open her stomach. She pulled out a small girl clearing her nose with a cloth and patting her back.

"What are you doing?!" Scarlet said crouched down next to her as the baby began to cry. She wrapped her in the same cloth and passed her too to Scarlet. "A baby is a baby" Elda whispered while quickly cutting the cord. She looked down and pulled another baby girl from Visha.

It did not cry. Her lips were blue, and her little body lay in her hands motionless. Elda rubbed her sternum hard with her fingers hard. She coughed up clear fluids and began to cry loudly. A sigh of relief came from her lips. Elda looked up at Scarlet. The girls looked around the room with wide eyes their thick black curly hair gleaming in the light.

"Now what? He will kill the both of them, and if Violet sees this!" Scarlet with her hands still full of babies looked at her sister in the bed. Elda stood up "Let me take care of this. It will be like they were never here." She took the girls from her arms. "Distract Niran. Take the baby to him to see." She said. "What are you going to do?" she asked worried looking at the twins. "Go." She whispered to her bouncing the newborns in her swaying arms trying to keep them quiet.

Hesitantly she left the room with the new prince. Elda worked fast cleaning her mess of bloody rags. She found a woven basket and placed the girls snugly inside closing the lid and then pilling the rags on top of it. "This." Elda paused looking around the room at the few left with her "This news goes nowhere. This shall never pass your lips or so help me no God will ever brig you peace.". They nodded in agreeance.

Elda paused next to Violet taking a moment to lean down and kiss her on the head "You did beautifully my dear.". She took Violets hand pinching her knuckle watching the skin slowly fall back down to the bone "She's dehydrated. Fetch some water.".

She walked into the hall with her arms full praying to herself the girls wouldn't make a sound. She passed

A Violet Night

Niran swooning over his new son lifting him into the light and with a joyous smile he looked to Elda "Will she be okay?". Elda nodded her head "She is exhausted, and probably has a concussion. Have the guards move her somewhere more comfortable and clean and we will get her washed up.". "Thank you" he mouthed to her turning his attention back to his son. She nodded again rushing out of the hallway. Just intime for the girls to start crying softly.

She walked into the kitchen closing and locking the door behind her. She quickly tore the lid off the basket looking at the now sleeping girls. She reached into the cabinet and grabbed two glass bottles placing it inside with them. Elda walked inside the connecting laundry room grabbing a two small wool pink blankets she rubbed their little heads as one cooed in her sleep "Do not you fear I will find you somewhere safe to go.".

A Violet Night

<u>Chapter 29.)</u>

Something cold splashed Violet in the face. She choked for air sitting up in the bed she was lying in. She looked around the room. Elda, Scarlet, and even Harriet had come to her side. She felt a warmth on her feet looking down to find Arrow stretching out. The smell of rotting copper filled her nose, and throbbing pain hit her lower half.

Harriet hugged her cousin "We thought you were dead.". "How long? How long have I been asleep like this?" She asked feeling her sore pains worsen. "You have been in and out for a three weeks now." Scarlet said sitting next to her. She looked down at her semi flattened stomach cautiously putting her hand on it. "And the baby?" She asked quietly.

"A healthy baby boy." Elda responded. Violet found her face slowly lighting up. "We had to find a wet nurse of course in the time being before your supply came in, but oh Violet, he is beautiful.". "May I see my son?" she asked trying to sit up farther.

Harriet and Scarlet helped her out of bed then down the hall. Her legs were weak. She could barely stand. Wobbling she entered the nursery. Niran stood over a small, rounded crib in the window. The two left Violet when they knew she could stand on her own and walked back out of the room.

Niran turned around surprised. He came taking her hand in his with a widening excited grin. "Come look at our son." He said eagerly. Gently he grabbed her arm with his free hand pulling her along swiftly.

Violet looked down at him sleeping, wrapped tightly in wool blankets, his platinum blonde hair peeking out of the top of the blanket. The baby opened his eyes and cooed at her. She couldn't keep her eyes off of him. An overwhelming feeling of comfort flushed through her.

She wanted very much to hate him. A very small part of her wanted to throw him out of the window and be done with it, but the more she looked at him the more her heart grew. This was her baby. She gave him life, and he was just as much a part of her as she was to him.

"Did you name him?" Violet asked letting the baby hold he finger. "Rowan." He said, "It was a strong name, for a strong surviving boy.". Violet felt her legs stumble a bit beneath her. She regained her balance carefully. Niran reached for her arm and helped her down in the rocking chair next to the crib.

He gently picked up Rowan and put him in her lap. "I will leave you to get to know each other." He said kissing him on the head and placing his hand on her shoulder tenderly before closing the two of them in the room alone.

He opened his bright blue eyes and let out a toothless smile. Her heart melted as she lifted him up to kiss him. His scent calmed her nerves. She hummed while rocking back and forth watching her baby drift back asleep.

She tightened her grip on him laying on her chest taking in the moment. This was her baby. This was her son. She pulled him back slightly and kissed his exposed head letting his little hair tickle her nose.

Violet laid him back down in his crib stroking his cheek with her fingers still humming the same tune Elda would to her when she was sick or in need of comfort. He was so soft and warm. So pure.

As she stood there watching him sleep she suddenly remembered the news Visha had told her. She felt uneasy and stumbled to the door opening it "Is it true?" She asked with sadness in her voice. Scarlet and Harriet stopped talking to one another and looked at her. "Well come on! Out with it. Is he dead?!" She asked feeling her face become flushed red. "Come, sit down with us." Harriet said calmly. "Just say it! Just tell me!" Her voice now growing more and more upset. Scarlet looked around with a conflicted look trying not to gaze into her upset eyes "Violet, Rory is dead.".

A silence filled the air "Vi,-" Harriet started to say. She put her hand up in the air "No. I do not want your condolences or your words. Just let me be alone with my thoughts.". Violet felt a void of black nothingness take hold of her body. She composed herself and walked to her room grabbing her cloak.

The thick snow had finished falling to the frozen ground. The wind burned her cheeks, and ears while she trudged her way through the knee deep white abyss. Her teeth chattered from inside her skull profoundly.

Violet felt with her numb fingers until she found the opening of the tunnel. She sat on the bed her fingers and toes purple and bright red stinging like a thousand pinpricks with the slight warmth inside of the cottage.

She had it cleaned for a little over a year now. Violet with the little energy that she had started a fire in the fireplace. Overtop lie the blue quilted blanket they had used on their picnic. She smiled unfolding it carefully taking in her memories. She held it to her face feeling the soft texture against her cheek. Walking back to the bed she flung it ver her body.

A Violet Night

"This was all just a bad dream...It had to be.." she thought to herself zoning out. A tear soft and warm perched on her cheek. She let out a hysteric laugh.. Rory must have come here before he left.. things looked just a little different inside. There was one of his bags on the table and glass jars of food in the cabinet. Even the bed had been made differently. She curled up farther in the blanket with a sniffle.

Laying there she saw the light reflect off of something on a shelf. Curious, she got up. It was a dagger. She sat at the table running her fingers along the inside of the blade collecting the dust off of it. She got to close to the end and pricked her finger. "Ouch." She said letting the blood drip to the floor.

Wheels began to turn in her head, *"I could end this. I could end this right here, right now."* She thought bringing the blade to her wrist. She pressed the blade to her skin enough to have a small trickle of blood run down. *"But what kind of a person will my son be without me?*" She

asked herself pulling the blade back from her wrist.

Suddenly her body was overtaken with rage. Violet

threw the dagger across the room with a loud cry. She

began to sob harder now hating herself for being so selfish.

She opened the door crusted with ice running out

into the blistering snow. She threw herself down. She

belted at the top of her lungs until her voice became

crackled and sore. "Why did you leave me?!" Her piercing

screams echoed off the rocks "Rory you promised!".

She laid down looking up to the grey clouds letting

the large snowflakes hit her in the face. "You promised.."

she whispered. Her tears now stung on her cheeks. She sat

up. The winds began to howl off the rocks surrounding her.

Violet body shivered.

Making her way back she laid down on the bed and

covered up with the blanket again ignoring the slight pain

in her wrist. She fell asleep hoping she would dream of Rory again, but she didn't dream at all. She awoke to her arms numb and cold. The fire had gone out while she was asleep. Violet sat up rubbing her arms together it was now dark outside. "*I need to get back to Rowan.*" She thought as she put her cloak back on slipping into her cold damp shoes.

Violet rushed back to the castle and into nursery. Rowan wasn't in his crib. She looked around the room this time studying it closely. Small wooden dolls and stuffed toys lined the walls on shelves. She smiled. Niran may be a monster, but he was a decent father from what she had seen.

She walked down the hall and knocked on Nirans chamber doors. "Come in." She heard him shout from the other side calmly. A small rocking cradle was sitting at the foot of his bed with Rowan inside. Niran sat at his table reading a few scripts. He took a hit off of his pipe and let the smoke rings roll off of his tongue as he spoke "How kind of you to grace your child with your presence again.".

Reality hit her. She reminded herself who he was to her. She walked over to the cradle and rubbed his head, smiling to herself. She took a moment to feel the fire on the back of her skin. "I do however give credit where credit is due. Given your record I thought I was going to have to kill the little bastard." He laughed generously.

She looked at him repulsed by his tone. He motioned her to come to him. Violet made her way and sat at the table next to him. She looked at the scripts layering the table. They were war letters from different captains including Conn, and other commanders. He watched her as she read over the papers. With his pipe tucked in his teeth he shuffled them into a pile and turned them face down.

"I got you something." Niran said blankly as he put a small red box on the table. She paused removing the lid to the box. Inside was a rose gold hand mirror with the most beautiful flowers carved into it, and a matching hairbrush with thick wired bristles.

"What is this for?" She asked setting the set back in the box. "As you lay in that bed almost more dead than alive I realized that you were more beautiful than I had originally perceived. Your flowing hair captivated me. I made the maidens brush your hair every morning and every evening when I was not available to do so. So it did not tangle.". *"How romantic."* She thought sarcastically.

He placed the mirror back into her hands gripping it tightly. "If you weren't so incredibly insecure you could do anything you wanted to Violet." He spoke letting go of her hands.

She looked at herself in the mirror maybe she had been too hard on herself. Her eyes wondered to the scars on her chest and sighed. The two purple scars protruded out of her dress. She rubbed them with her fingers tracing the uneven skin. They were rough and ridged now. "I wish she hadn't of done that where people could see it." He said rubbing his thumb against the right scar lightly leaning in against the table.

"Your chest once beautiful, now so ugly. A pity really." He said pulling her dress up over them. "I suppose you need your rest.." He said realizing this was too much for her to take in for the night. Violet nodded looking at the baby getting up from the table. "You know you could stay in here tonight with us… I won't try anything. Truth is I need help with him. I need your help, and I just don't feel right letting other people take care of him.". Violet didn't know how to respond. He studied her uneasiness "We can even use separate covers if you would like.".

He walked over to his wardrobe and grabbed one of his oversized shirts. He laid it out on neatly on the bed "You should get cleaned up. It looks like you have had quite the evening.". She walked to the bed stopping in front of it. He came up behind her and gently untied her soaking wet cloak from around her neck taking it off of her shoulders. She jumped when he touched her. "Relax. I am only trying to help you." He said looking at her bloody arm. She pulled her arm out of view tucking it against her side "I do not, nor have I ever needed your help Niran. Not now or ever.". "Violet it's nothing I haven't already seen of you." He said raising his eyebrow at her.

She reluctantly peeled off her wet dress and pulled on his shirt that stopped just above her knees. He ushered her to sit on the edge of the bed "Let me see." He said holding a long clean bandage in his lap, a small towel, and a bottle of alcohol in his hand. "If it's not cleaned it will fester." He said grabbing her arm and pulling it across his lap. She leaned with his jerk. Violet watched as he carefully poured the alcohol over her wound. She let out a hiss.

"Stop your wiggling." He said dapping it dry with the towel. He bandaged it tightly folding her arm up to make sure he didn't cut off her circulation. "Thank you." She said looking at him as he put his things away.

He nodded his head "You should get some rest.". Without another word Violet picked up her son and laid in the bed cradling him in her arms. Niran covered them both with a soft black wool blanket. For once Violet actually smiled back at him "Thank you." She whispered again to him. He rubbed her head softly "As far as the accident on your wrist goes you do not have to explain anything to me.". He sat back at his table continuing on with his work. Looking up occasionally at them on the bed.

A Violet Night

Chapter 30.)

The camp was filled with large cream colored tents all filled to the rising brim with solders. Rory took his helmet off wiping the dirt from his face. He walked into his own tent with Lee and 12 other men all having their separate conversations.

He sat down on the ground with his back propped against a wooden crate. He crossed his arms letting his head tip back behind him and began to fall asleep.

Over the past few weeks Rory had gotten used to all of the noise of the men playing cards, telling their stories all too loud, and sharpening their swords, arrows, and spears.

"Guerrero." A voice from the other side of the tent walls. His eyes flickered open. Tired as he was he stood back up. He peeled open the thin tent wall entrance to the cool breeze. There was no one standing in front of him confused he looked to his left; a small slander man stood with his hands behind his back. Rory let his body relax. The man nodded looking beyond him.

A bag was thrown over his head. He swung his fist without aim hoping to hit his attackers. The little man let out a snicker as he struck in the back of the head. Rory could hear a ringing in his ears. His body crumbled to the damp ground.

Rory awoke to darkness. The bag was still over his head. His head was throbbing. He went to rub his head, but soon realized his hands were bound in cold shackles. "*Son of a bitch."* He thought shaking his head slightly with a smirk.

A sharp kick to the stomach took his breath away. The bag was then ripped off of his head. The sudden burst of light made his vision blurry. He tried to blink his vision back to normal. "I was beginning to think you would never wake up handsome." A familiar voice coated his ears.

Rory squinted his eyes. A woman was hovering over him playing with his hair. He pulled his head away from her. She took a step back smiling at him. He squinted harder "Visha?" He choked out quietly. "What are you-". She cut him off "What am I doing?". He looked at her confused. Niran slipped though the tent opening. "Why am I here?" Rory asked pulling on his bound hands.

"Let us kill him now." She begged. He scoffed, "No, I think I want him alive. In fact, I need him alive. I want to see the pain in his face every day." He said smiling at Rory. He squatted in front of him becoming eye level.

"But you said-" Visha whined. "Shut your mouth women."

He said growled growing angry with her. "I see why you

got bored of her and her loudmouth." He joked with Rory

"Yes, I see why you left her for such a *softer* woman.. So

tender, so wet between her thighs." Rory kicked at him just

barely getting his leg. He laughed amused before punching

him. Rory looked passed Niran at Visha. She looked at her

feet he could tell what Niran said was hurting her.

He grabbed a fistful of Rory's hair forcing him to

look him in the eyes again squatting at his level yet again

"That was the same energy Violet had the night I first had

her. Of course now that she bares my heir I cannot beat her

as hard as I want too.". Rory looked up at him shocked his

heart felt like a bag of rocks in water. Nirans eyes lightened

as he chuckled. "You hadn't heard? Although if it does

come out to be yours, I suppose I'll have to send it to you."

He paused "Piece by piece of course, you would get the little bastard.".

"If you hurt her I'll kill you!" He shouted trying to stand bearing his weight against the tent support pole. Niran laughed "I am untouchable.". He tapped on Rory's chin with his pointer finger.

Niran stood up. "Take him to the holding cells." He told a guard as he smiled at Rory patting his head aggressively. He walked to Visha pausing to smile at her as if he was going to say something else before leaving the tent. Visha turned slowly to follow. "Visha wait. Why are you doing this to me?" He asked full of sorrow and anger.

Visha turned around facing him "You broke me Rory.. Why her? Why not me? She is everything I could never be for you." She said holding back tears in her eyes. "Visha I-" He started. "Stop." She said drying her face quickly with her sleeve. "You reap what you sew. You should have stayed with what you had. Why wasn't I good enough for you Ri? I kept you company all of those nights, I pleasured you when no one else would. I guess it doesn't matter now you made your bed and now you must lie in it. Now you must lie in it and cry yourself to sleep the way I did the night I walked in on you two. I want you to feel your heart rip apart the way I did when you forgot about me for something newer. When you replaced me with her.".

Rory let his body sink a little farther down. His eyes softened a bit "I never meant to hurt you." He said softly "I cannot tell you what it is about her that is so engulfing. I just fell in love with her. It all happened so fast... I am sorry for the way things turned out.". "As you should be." She said bitterly slipping out of the tent.

The guards unshackled him walking him out into the daylight. "Rory?" Lee asked confused from his group of chattering comrades. Rory let out a boyish smile and waved one hand to him. "Move along." One of the guards said shoving him ahead. They tossed him into a small makeshift stone holding room in another building. There was a small blanket on the dirt floor, and flies buzzed around him at the stench of the room.

He threw his back against the wall and cupped his hands over his mouth. He had never felt this angry, this bitter. *"How could she? How could she have his spawn?"*. He kicked his metal drinking cup, it hit the iron bars with a loud bang.

The cell door creaked open breaking Rory's thoughts. Visha stood hanging the key back into the wall "Go Ri before I change my mind… Go.." He looked at her confused before standing up and slowly creeping near her. "The guards are all a dinner, you are the only prisoner in here. They won't be checking on you until in the morning, so please go.".

A Violet Night

She moved closer to him in the cell, "Are you fucking stup-". He cut her off by grabbing her by the throat and shoving her against the wall. Her face was turning red as she grasped at his hand desperately. Now standing on her tiptoes she managed to gasp out "I. Deserve.... This.". He dropped her to the floor as she held her neck chocking for air. He helped her back onto her feet. He looked into her eyes still full of rage. "I am sorry too Rory." She said lightly.

He studied her hard breathing looking down at her chest and kissed her with great force. Surprised as she was she kissed him back guiding his hands up her dress. She wasn't wearing anything underneath. He quickly pulled his pants down and picked her up against the wall entering her warm body. She moaned loudly. He covered her mouth with one hand as she bit his fingers.

He finished inside of her. Setting her down he helped her readjust before pulling up his own pants and leaving the cell. He thought of Violet and for a minute he felt guilty for his actions.

"If you go behind this building directly into the woods no one will see you escape." She said pulling herself together. "What about Lee?" He asked looking at her carefully. "I will make sure they bring him back before he even sees a battle. He is my friend too.. I wouldn't want him to get hurt" She said. "Thank you, but what will you tell people of me?" He said looking back at the cell. "Once they notice you have gone missing they will not want to tell Niran. They will declare you dead. I have already spoken to a few guards regarding to your broken heartedness." He nodded at her sincerely before darting out of the door.

"Do not forget this." He heard a voice from behind the building. His uncle threw his bag at him already packed with a change of clothes. "How?" Rory asked confused looking all around to make sure no one was watching. "Relax.. She warned me of her plan.. I will do my best to cover for your death story." He chewed the inside of his

chapped lip "Go.. Go on before someone catches you. I will

find you when things die down around here." He said

placing his hands on his buckle. "Thank you.." He mouthed

to him. He nodded at him and patted his shoulder "Now go

on. Get!".

A Violet Night

Chapter 31.)

Without hesitation Rory started back for Violet. He had to see it for himself. He had to know that she was safe at the least. With no stops he made it to the kingdom in a week. His legs were sore from all the walking, only stopping briefly to sleep when he could and find a drink of water.

He peeked into the kitchen window. Elda was leaning against the wall trying to regain her thoughts. He tapped on the glass with the knuckle of his middle finger and darted behind the door. He could hear her soft swift footsteps coming close as she creaked open the rounded door curiously poking her head out.

He let out a smile and leaned down to hug the old woman. She embraced it for only a moment before slapping the back of his head. "What are you doing here.?!" She pulled his hood back over his head and rushed him inside. "If he sees you here he will kill you!". "Have you no faith?" He said with a wink at her pouring himself a large glass of water. "I just need to see here Elda. I just need to know she is safe.".

Elda wrinkled her forehead before letting out a sigh. She refilled his glass with water. He looked at her graciously chugging it again letting it dribble out of the corners of his mouth. "You know it may not be his child." She said drying his face with her pocket cloth. He avoided the thoughts pushing them aside in his head. "Don't get caught Rory." She said opening the conjoining linen room.

She grabbed a guard uniform one with a masked face per Nirans new design.

He headed down the hall silently worried someone might recognize his stride. There she was. Walking down the hall both hands on her very small round belly. His heart fluttered with raw emotion. He wanted to run up to her and scoop her out of this mess. He smiled to himself. Her body stiffened up as Niran approached her. They were speaking, but he couldn't make out the words. Rory tried his best to look busy. She broke a small smile at Niran. He kissed her head and then her belly and continued to walk down the hall on the opposite direction.

She began to walk towards him now. He was enraged. *"How could she be happy?!"* His mind drifted and without warning he bumped into her. He reached out his arms to catch her. "I am so sorry." She whispered now crying. His inner voice was shouting *"TAKE OFF YOUR MASK!"*.

Defying everything inside of himself he nodded his head dropping her arms. She stood there for a moment before wiping away her own tears with her sleeve. "I know how silly of me.. I should be happy right?" She laughed rubbing her belly again "Anyways, I am sorry again." She said walking away.

He watched her following behind her silently at a good distance she walked to her room. "You don't look well." Elda said coming up to her. Violet shook her head "Never better.". Elda wrinkled her raised eyebrows at her pulling her in for a hug "Come now, I will make you some broth." She looked over Violets head and down the hall to Rory. He shook his head at her softly while she ushered her into her room.

He waited until it was dark watching over her all day silently throughout the halls. "She is fine in here." He said to himself cleaning out his old room into two small separate bags. "Who am I to take her away from this life?"

He asked himself. "Who am I to raise a child? I cannot give them the world they need. That they deserve.".

Elda opened his door. "I thought I might find you down here." She said with a lantern light in her hands. "Tell her nothing of this. Please Elda I beg of you. They are better off without me. I cannot give them the world as he can.".

She grabbed at his hands and nodded. "But you do not know unless you try.." she spoke softly. "I will not stop watching over her. I will come through time to time and check on them as they grow into their new selves, but I cannot stay here.".

"Elda I-" Scarlets voice echoed through the room as she covered her mouth. Rory closed the door behind her "He's not staying." Elda said placing her hand up to her. "WHY NOT?" she said angrily. "I cannot give them anything they deserve!" He exerted trying to explaining himself again to them this time getting louder. "Rory-".

"No. You and I both know that I cannot give them the world that I want to! This is safer for them here. A life on the run? With a child non the less." He said throwing his hands behind his head overwhelmed with all the possible decisions he could make. Scarlet nodded understanding where he was coming from.

"Did you see her?" She asked trying to calm him. He looked at her taking a deep breath "She is even more beautiful than the memories I have kept.". "So stay." She asked of him. "If I stay I will only want to save her for my own selfish needs.. It is better this way. For her and her child.".

"Do you have somewhere to stay at least?" Elda asked picking up his bag for him and sliding it on his shoulder. "I have a place in mind. It is hidden and out of sight." He said quickly. "I will go ahead and pack you some supplies to last a few weeks if you ration it properly." She grabbed Scarlets hand "Come." She said leading her out of the room. "You are wrong you know.. She does need you.." Scarlet said peering back in at him before disappearing with Elda.

Rory nodded at her. Elda tugged at her hand "Come now child.".

A Violet Night

Chapter 32.)

"Awow." Rowan giggled as the he ran across the room chasing the dog. Violet laughed at her son as he tripped over his own two feet. She bent down and picked him up placing him on her lap.

A smile leaked out of her lips looking at each other in the mirror. She ruffled up his curly hair and let the wiggly toddler down. She still couldn't believe he was already almost two years of age now. She looked back at herself running her fingers through her hair undoing her long braid.

A Violet Night

Life had gotten slightly better for her. Violet had succumbed to the circumstances. She no longer had her own quarters. She sleeps with Nirans in *their* chambers, and her old chambers now served as an overflow of storage for Rowans belongings.

Niran opened the doors. Violet looked at her hands in her lap as he made his way towards them. He looked at her in the mirror and his frown turned into a smile. The toddler waddled to him arms spread out. Violet watched them in the mirror her heart full of disgust as he touched their child. Picking him up into the air and hugging him tightly.

He cradled Rowan's chubby face in his hands. "Look at your mommy." He said making the toddler laugh at the tone of his voice. Violet dug her nails into the palm of her hands. She let out a deep sigh. He grinned at her anger. "I will see you tonight at the dinner table." She said standing up reaching for their child.

A Violet Night

He pulled away slightly looking at her curiously. "You know Violet, my appetite is for something other than food tonight." He grinned devilishly at her.

His eyes suddenly changed "Why do you still hate me?" he asked. Violet waited to respond, "Would you have treated Ann the way you do to me?". He shook his head hard "No. I-I do not know what it is about you that makes me treat you in this way. Sometimes it is just too overwhelming for me not to treat you in this manner.".

Violet wasn't sure how to answer him, "There was a time very long ago that I was delighted for you to be a part of this family... Though I never imagined it would be in this way. Do better for him. Fight the urge Niran." She said looking at their child. He opened his mouth to speak again she could tell he wanted to say something hateful or sarcastic but instead he said, "I was wrong to bring this up in front of little ears.". She nodded in agreeance with him.

A Violet Night

She took Rowan from his arms and walked towards to doors. "I will see you here tonight after dinner. Wear nothing and leave Rowan with Elda. We have some catching up to do my Queen.". She paused turning around to him. "No Niran." She said profoundly. "No?" He asked with a smirk. "I am allowed to say no." She looked at him sternly. He came closer. Violet tightened her grip on Rowan. She gulped as he smiled in her face forcefully pulling Rowan out of her arms. He placed him on the ground and patted him on the head. Turning towards her his smile faded.

"Allowed to say no?" Niran snatched his hands around her throat scaring Rowan into tears. She flinched while his face came closer. He shoved her against the wall hitting her head against it. A deep low growl illuminated from Arrows jowls. She slowly embedded herself in between the two. He kicked her hard in the ribs, she stumbled off yelping towards Rowan.

A Violet Night

"I am in charge around here. You do as I say... You made me kill my plaything if you don't recall. All I have left is you now." He said looking straight into her eyes "You are quite lucky he is in here, or I would have already had you on your back.".

By now she could feel the blood gushing to her face. He smiled and leaned into her ear. "It has been a long time since this fire has ignited in you my dear. I have longed for it." He whispered. She tried to push his hands off of her neck. He squeezed tighter.

She could barely hear Rowan crying over her own heartbeat in her temples. He licked her bottom lip biting it gently "I will have you tonight my Queen." He dropped her to the floor. Her body fell heavily. She gasped for air while she scrambled to pick up her son bringing him close to her body. She forced herself to calm down for him.

"You'll spoil that boy." He said opening the doors to the hallway "The red in your face really brings out your eyes." He said leaning down brushing the hair out of her face. She jerked away stumbling to her feet and out of the door. Arrow following close behind. Her vision was still hazy doing her best to comfort her son her and find her way back to her old room.

"Are you alright your highness?" A voice called out to her. "Yes I- I am just not feeling myself today." She said to the woman holding a basket of clean sheets. The women shifted her balance looking at Violets swollen red neck. "May I see you to wherever you are going?" She asked. "I think I will manage but thank you for your concern." Violet said trying to cover her neck with Rowan head. She tried to give a reassuring smile to her as she continued on her way.

She physically and mentally could not make it to her old room. Her body, and mind were tired. She settled for Scarlets room. Letting herself in and closing the door behind her. It was empty and quiet. She kissed Rowen on the side of his head shifting him to her other hip.

Arrow nudged herself through her legs. She squatted down putting her head to the dogs and closing her eyes "It's okay." She whispered out loud "We are going to be okay.".

A Violet Night

Chapter 33.)

She laid on the bed in Scarlets room with her confused and upset son. Her arms saturated in salty tears and snot. Her throat was soar as she tried to swallow. "Shhhhh…Shhhhhh…Shhhh…" She said rocking him in her arms until he drifted off into a dream.

She ran her fingers through his blonde hair tracing his freckles on the bridge of his small nose before using his shirt to wipe it. She peeled his little sweaty head off of her arm and gently down on the pillow. She carefully slipped out of the bed.

A Violet Night

She looked at herself in the mirror running her fingers over her bruised neck and down unto her scared chest. She gripped where her dress sat on her shoulders.

How did she let this happen to herself? How did she become so weak? Why did she not leave with Rory when she had the chance. *"Rory..."* Violet thought again. She smiled at herself dropping her hands to her sides.

She went to the shelf and grabbed the red book sitting down at the vanity and pulled out his note. She read it again slowly savoring every sweet word in his handwriting trying her best to remember his voice as if it were flowing through her ears in the moment. His voice was but a ghost whisper in her ears now.

The door opened as she pushed the note down in her lap quickly. Arrow jumped into a defensive position. "Relax." Scarlet said taking her maid apron off and tossing it on the bed. She giggled amongst herself as it covered up

A Violet Night

Rowan. She pulled it off the sleeping baby and looked up making eye contact with Violet in the mirror. Her eyes and voice become concerned "Did he do that to you?". She began reaching to touch her neck slowly. "It is nothing, really. It's okay.. he doesn't usually do this anymore.." She stuttered pushing her hand away trying to turn her body away.

The note fell out of her lap floating to the floor. Violet bumped her knee off the corner of the vanity trying to grab it. She became flustered taking a deep breath in. Her face became flushed she reached down to pick it up. A single tear drop fell from her nose as she bent over.

Scarlet crouched down next to her pulling her arms into hers placing the fallen note I her hands "No. No, Violet it's not okay. Do you want him to see this every day? Do you want him to be his father?". Violet looked at her baby sleeping in the bed. "Of course you don't." She whispered looking at her nephew in the mirror.

"Scarlet, he is his father.. there is nothing I can do to change that." Violet said pulling her arms back to her lap clutching Rory's note. "Do you want to end up like Visha? I am more than sure she thought she was untouchable just as you do now.. He is manic. Mad even. He changes his mood in seconds with no warning.." Scarlet said grabbing her sisters wrist tightly. A small uneasy smile perched on her lips "I have a plan.".

"No. No. No. He will murder all of us all for even having such thoughts." Violet said with a tremble in her voice. "Just trust me. It will all work out." She said not breaking eye contact. "What are you going to do?" She asked. "The less you know the better it will be for you and baby boy." Scarlet stood up crossing her arms and looking at the remainder of light outside before running to the bed and tying her apron back around her waist rushing out of the room.

A Violet Night

Violet looked down and loosened her grip on the note nodding to reassure herself. She put the note away and stood over her sleeping son. It calmed her in the mist of her confusion and worry to watch his small chest rise and fall.

"We will get through this. That I promise you, even if it is the last thing I do." She thought to herself laying back down next to Rowan. Arrow jumped on the bed laying her head on Violets side the dog let out a huff and closed her eyes. She ran her hand across her head softly "Good girl." She whispered dozing off herself.

"Hungy mommy." Rowan mumbled pushing on his moms face. Violet cracked her eyes open to her smiley baby. She looked to the window. It was now almost night fall. Taking her hand she wiped the drool from the side of her face. "Ouchy mommy, Ouchy." He said pointing to her neck. "Yes baby, mommy has an ouchy." She said playing with his hands. He smiled and began to hug Arrow. *"How*

did I get lucky enough to have such a smart, sweet boy?"
She thought to herself.

She proceeded to clean herself and Rowan up for dinner. "Ewda?" Rowan said tugging on his moms dress. "We'll go see miss Elda." She said fastening her earing, looking down at him as he grinned ear to ear. "Wace mommy, wace, wace!" He said reaching on his tip toes, with his pudgy hand to the door handle.

She opened the door for him and watched him teetertotter down the hallways letting out high pitch screeches of joy. She giggled to herself, then began to jog behind him "Oh no, Row. Looks like you won." She said scooping his little body up in her arms and swinging him around. He began to laugh. She looked up at the counter her eyes met with Elda's and Scarlets. They looked scared and worried as their voices became hushed.

A Violet Night

She set her son down with a pat on the behind letting his walk around the room. She anxiously looked at them both rubbing her sweaty palms down her sides.

There were two small brown cork topped vials on the countertop. Violet corrected her posture "So this is your plan then?" She whispered angrily "He is no mere idiot.". She looked at her son playing with a broom in the corner. "It is abundantly simple, yes. But very effective. Besides we have no other alternative Vi.. He has lowered his guard with us in this time." Scarlet said.

"I think this is a bad idea.. I want nothing to do with this child, you hear me? Nothing!" Elda said sternly picking up Rowan. He wrapped his little arms around her neck. She walked out into the garden with him mumbling "Let's go pick some tomatoes.". "Yeah!" He said with excitement.

A Violet Night

Scarlet scooped the vials into her apron pocket and turned to Violet "We don't have to go through with this.". "I know." Violet said pausing "I'm scared.". Scarlet bit her tongue nervously as she shoved Violet towards the door "Now go, the less you see me do the better. Just act normal at dinner tonight and have faith in me sister.".

"If something goes wrong promise me Scarlet. Promise me that you will take Rowan and go to the hidden cottage I described to you.". She nodded her head "But nothing will happen, and everything will be fine. Have faith… Now go. Go collect yourself while Rowan is occupied.".

Violet looked out the window. Elda made Rowan wave at her. They were swirling around in the sunlight. She smiled at them making her think about her own childhood spent with her. She waved back at them "Go." Elda mouthed to Violet kissing him on the cheek.

She turned back to Scarlet "He is fine, now get out

of here." She said shoving her out of the room. "Alright,

alright." Violet said letting her close the door in her face.

She made her way to their chamber. Violet opened

the door praying for him to not be inside. "Where is our

son?" His graveled voice pierced her ears. He stood in front

of the elongated mirror slipping the sleeves of his shirt on

without buttoning it he turned around to face her.

"With Elda cooking dinner." She said unable to

look into his eyes. "Good. A boy should know how to

cook." He said fixing his cufflinks as he folded back his

sleeves to his elbows.

His hair was a mess. She had never not seen it not

done before. She walked to the chair at the table placing her

hands on the top. He looked down at her fixating on her

neck and sighed. "I am sorry for my temper in front of

Rowen." He said staggering with his motions. He began to

button the bottom half of his shirt. He was nervous about something. He motioned her to sit as he pulled the chair out for her.

"You know... Violet I didn't kill your sister. As much as you would love to pin that one on me. I loved her you know?" He said looking up at her wide eyed. "Then who did? Why did you not come forward? My parents begged you for information surrounding her death." She said looking up at him. He stood almost on top of her now.

"Just know I got justice for her, and your family that day." He said softy tracing her bruised neck with one of his hands moving her hair slightly. Violets body shook as his fingers pulled away from her. She was confused on how she felt. "Your mother.. She did it.. That explains her death." She whispered putting the pieces together for herself. He looked up with an uneasy smile and an exhausted empty laugh "There was no length I would not have gone for her. I need you to know that… I will do unspeakable things for the ones I love.".

He cupped her chin making her look up at him softly "I truly am sorry for the ways in which you make me treat you.". She looked up blankly her heart beat a little faster.

He leaned one hand on the top of the back of the chair and the other on the base next to her thigh. She could smell his breath, it smelled of peppermint. He was inches from her now, their eyes locked onto one another.

"I know I will never be him, but maybe you could pretend just this once that I was." He said leaning in kissing her softly. She kissed him back putting one hand on the side of his face. Violet was caught in an internal battle with herself. Niran picked her up out of the chair and laid her on the bed.

A Violet Night

She kept her eyes closed trying to envision Rory on top of her as he kissed and undressed her body. She was disgusted at herself for enjoying this moment with him.

A Violet Night

<u>Chapter 34.)</u>

Pushing the last pin into her hair Violet stepped away from the mirror. Niran watched from over her shoulder leaning against the bed rail. "I will see you downstairs." He said kissing her hand with a small bow. She pulled it back to her side shaking with guilt. She took a deep breath in and exhaled.

"Calm down, everything will be alright." She thought to herself. Drifting her way downstairs a couple minutes after he had left her alone in the room. Her mind and her heart began to race with doubt. *"What if everything goes wrong? Or what happens if it works?"*.

A Violet Night

She sat down at the table across from Niran. Rowan was sitting in his lap. "Tell me something Violet." He said breaking her train of thought. She looked at him wondering if he too could hear her heartbeat in her throat.

"What do you think about bearing me another?" He asked. *"Is he joking? Is he really asking me this right now?"* She thought to herself. She then let out a forced smile nodding "To the future." She said raising her glass in the air. He raised his in the air alongside hers grinning ear to ear.

Scarlet, Elda, and two other girls began to bring out the bowls of tomato soup, and loaves of fresh soft baked bread. Elda placed a bowl in front of Violet not making eye contact with her. She moved down the table and began to pick up Rowan from Nirans lap. The boy squirmed and snuggled up to Nirans chest. "He may stay." He said sharply.

A Violet Night

Elda moved Rowans bowl closer to him. She looked up at Violet now concerned handing him his tiny spoon. Violet caught on to her glare. "You don't want him to spill that on you dear, it's hot and you know he eats like a barbarian.". Niran chuckled and motioned for Elda to bring a chair closer sliding his little body into the other chair. Violet let out a silent sigh of relief.

Scarlet slid the bowl in front of him "I hope you like it my King.". He scoffed "Finally learned some manners huh?". "Something like that." She said with a grin. Violet gripped the end of her seat wishing Scarlet would shut her mouth.

He picked up his spoon and dipped it into the bowl. The steam hovered over the spoon "Bite. Bite." Rowan said looking at his father. He smiled and began to bring the spoon to his lips. "He needs to eat his own food. We are all eating the same thing, in your own words 'You spoil him'."

Violet said anxiously. He paused pulling back slightly and rolled his eyes at her.

He continued to move the spoon towards Rowan. "Let me feed him for you." Elda said standing in between the spoon and Rowan with his toddler sized portion in her hands.

Niran raised an eyebrow at Violet then to Elda. "Where is the kitchen whore?" He asked looking around. Scarlet came around the corner nervously. "Taste my food." He said calmly. "But your grace I-" She said looking frantic. "Taste. The. Fucking. Food. I did not think that I stuttered." He said raising his voice at her pushing to bowl towards her spilling a little on the white tablecloth.

She hesitated. He put his hand out palm up towards the bowl. Scarlets hand shook as she weaved the spoon in between her fingers. "Eat." He said leaning back in his chair calmly. "I-" Scarlet whimpered looking at the bowl.

"For fucks sake. Someone eat it!" He shouted impatiently sitting up again. Without a pause Elda stepped in and took the spoon from Scarlet placing it in her mouth. Violet bit her tongue watching in horror from across the table. She set the spoon down "Swallow." He said biting his tongue amused. She gulped the liquid down "Taste like soup". His posture softened still watching cautiously. She pushed the bowl back over to Niran glancing between the two of them.

Elda grabbed Scarlets arm to turn and walk away. "All of it. Eat all of it." He pushed the bowl once more. "This is ridiculous Niran. Eat your dinner. You are simply paranoid." Violet said. He didn't take his eyes off of the pair only raised his hand to Violets commentary.

"Do it or I will feed it to them." He said. Elda and Scarlet walked back to the table. "There is nothing wrong with your food my King. I assure you I only have a tomato allergy." Scarlet reassured him. He shrugged his shoulders and folded his fingers together "Prove me wrong then. Fuel my humor.".

Elda looked at Violet and then took the bowl into her hands. "Put it down." Violet said standing up. Niran shot Violet a look. Elda took out the spoon and sipped it pulling it away from her face. He shook his head and lifted the bowl to her with his two fingers "Finish it.". Elda paused took a deep breath in then began to chug down the soup. She set the bowl down again turning around to walk out of the room. "Do stay." He insisted now kicking his chair back and putting his boots on the corner of the table. "Is this really necessary Niran?" Violet asked him. With a smirk "Can never be too careful my love. Have a seat Elda." He said reaching past his own glass taking a drink of Rowan juice.

Long moments past of them exchanging silent glances "May I be excused?" Elda stood up quickly. "No you may not." He said placing his feet firmly back onto the floor leaning in intrigued. She did her best to try expeditiously to walk out of the room.

Her back became hunched as she grabbed her stomach and began to throw up violently. It was white, pink, thick, and frothy. Niran began to laugh grabbing at his stubbly facial hair leaning in to watch her on all fours howling in pain.

Violet ran over to her. Scarlet covered her mouth in horror. Elda collapsed on the floor blood poured out of her eyes, nose, ears, and mouth as her body shook with great force in her arms. Violet turned her head to the side in her lap in hopes she would not choke. She coughed and a more white frothy foam slowly leaked from the corner of her lips. Her body stopped convulsing, and her breathing stopped.

Violet began to cry cradling the women who raised her in her arms. She watched her chest as she shook her begging for her to breathe. The light in her eyes was gone. Elda was dead.

Niran stood up from his chair and struck Scarlet across the face with the back of his hand. "You really thought you could get away with such a weak attack?" He said with a laugh. Scarlet spit onto the floor with no time to react. Still with a grin he picked her up by the base of her skull. Scarlet struggled against him clawing at his face and hands trying to pry them apart. "I have waited far too long for this day to come." He said placing his opposite hand on her neck squeezing harder.

Scarlets hands became limp at her sides. Violet panicked picking up a bottle of wine off of the table she quickly smashed it against the back of Nirans head. They both dropped to the ground. Scarlet gasped for air holding her neck with her own hands terrified.

"Get up! There is no time for feelings! Here!"

Violet said picking her up off the ground. Glass crunched

beneath her heels. She ran to Rowan picking him up and

tossing him to her sister "I'll meet you at the safe place.

Now go.". She gave her a shove. "But-" Scarlet said still

out of breath. "For fucks sake! Go!" She shouted standing

over Nirans unconscious body. He was making muffled

moaning sounds.

"Leave Violet, just leave with them!" A voice inside

her screamed loudly. She shook her head *"No... I am only*

just beginning.". She tied up his hands behind his back and

feet with some thick course rope off the wall curtains. His

eyes fluttered open looking at her dazed and confused. She

panicked stuffing his mouth with a cloth napkin and tying

another tightly around his head.

Violet walked back to Elda. "I am so sorry." She

whispered to her. She propped her against a pillar propping

her hands on her stomach. Taking own her two fingers she closed Eldas eyes for the last time.

A Violet Night

<u>Chapter 35.)</u>

Violet looked around the room. There was no way she could drag him to a bedroom without being spotted. She could hear distant voices echoing throughout the hallways ahead. "Fuck." She whispered. Her eyes wondered past his squirming body and onto Elda's corpse.

"The kitchen." She thought to herself. She quickly did her best struggling to drag him to the kitchen closing the door and locking it behind her. Then rushing to lock the top and the bottom of the back door to the garden. She leaned against the wall to catch her breath "You know, you

sure are a big man for me to be carrying you around like that.".

Violet pulled him so that his back was now siting against the cabinets. His eyes were filled with rage and his mouth was filled with muffled slurs. She stretched her back pressing her thumbs into her spine until she felt it pop. A shimmer of light reflection caught her attention.

She smiled grabbing a knife from the countertop. She ran her finger across the blade and stopped at the point. Niran kicked his feet at her. She hiked up her dress and straddled his lap.

Running the flat side of the knife across his cheek bones and jaw line he pulled his head away. "Shhh…There. There." She said tenderly grabbing his jaw with her free hand forcing him to look into her eyes. She could hear all of the names he was calling her in his head. It made her feel in charge.

A Violet Night

"I think I get it." She said studying over his face.

She tapped the tip of blade down beside her. "I now

understand why you do what you do to people Niran. It's a

surge of power in my flesh I have never known.". She

traced her bare hands down his neck giving him

goosebumps. She began to unbutton his shirt slowly,

stopping at the bottom and pulling it open exposing his

chest. She could feel him get hard in between her legs. She

gave him a disgusted look picking up the knife once more.

Violet leaned into his neck making sure to breath

heavy. "A Queen should always be a part of her King,

don't you think?" She whispered in his ear seductively. He

nodded eagerly. She looked at her reflection in the blade

before looking back at him "Good. I am truly glad you

agree.". She began to carve into his chest with the blade.

He grunted and thrashed in pain. She forced herself to

buckle down her weight in her hips and legs trying her best

to keep him in the same spot. She stood up and took a step

back admiring her handywork. "Do not worry dear. It's only my name. Now I'll always be with you, now and forever. Isn't that what you wanted?".

A knock at the door and a jangle of keys interrupted her scattering her thoughts. Violet darted in front of it as the door cracked open dropping the knife on the ground with a 'clank' in front of Nirans feet. "Oh, my Queen." A servant said looking at the floor. "I am currently punishing a new scullery maid. Unless you want to be the next let me attend to my business." She slammed the door in the girls face relocking the door. Violet paced back and forth around the kitchen. *"Fresh air."* She thought. She cracked open both parts of the garden door *"Let me finish this and be on my way.".*

She took a deep breath of the air, her anxiety of being caught was now at an all-time high. She heard a sudden blood curdling scream from inside. Someone had found Elda.

A Violet Night

She felt her body being slammed through the door face first into the fresh mud she caught herself with her hands barely. Her body was tossed back around like a doll in a child's hands. Niran pinned her to the ground. She struggled trying the push him off. "You are stronger than I remember dear." He smiled. "Though, you should have just ended my life and moved on. Or tied the restraints a bit tighter. You know I have always had a thing for bondage with you Violet." He winked at her enjoying the moment.

She scratched his face and neck with her nails. He pushed his weight through his hands into her wrist. "Violet where is our son?" He asked calmly. "I will never tell you." She growled as she felt his warm blood drip down onto her. He sighed "I just do not know how I can let you live even if you were not a part of this." He pulled on her bringing one of her wrist to her other now pinning them back with one hand above her head and punched her in the ribs.

A Violet Night

She gasped not from the pain but from trying to catch her breath. "We can do this the easy way, or my favorite way." He said now surrendering all of his weight sitting on top of her lower chest preventing her from filling her lungs all the way. "I cannot bring myself to remember our last exciting rendezvous like this my dear. I was beginning to think you had lost your flame." He said leaning face to face with her.

Niran grunted in pain as weight came off of her chest as she gasped for air rolling to her side. She looked to her left, Arrow had a hold of Nirans arm. She was growling as he flung her body around with his arm trying the get her off. Violet managed to stumble to her feet slipping out of her shoes and began running into the tree line. She could hear Arrow yelp loudly in the distance, and then silence. She did her best not to turn around.

Violet ran fast stumbling around trying to regain her stamina tripping on sharp rocks as thorns and Xanthium plants that pierced her feet with every step. Using her core memory she ran until she thought she was going to pass out. She could see the entrance stone to the cottage in the distance. She slowed down trying to slow her breathing. The adrenaline was wearing off.

She glanced down at her feet. They were sore with cuts and bruises. She squatted down and pulled off a piece of Xanthium that was imbedded in her skin. She flicked it off her finger, it tried to stick to her skin with its sharp needle like edges. The sky rumbled. Dark clouds drifted in over the setting sun. The wind became cool on her skin. She began to step painfully towards the entrance.

The rain began to weep heavily to the ground. She lost sight in front of her. The rain bounced off of every surface around her. She put her hands out to her sides and began to laugh hysterically feeling the large raindrops hit her face. Lightning flashed across the sky. She counted the second in between until the thunder rustled the ground below her feet telling her how far away the storm was. She thought of Elda and the first time she brought her outside during a storm to feel the earth erupt. She was grateful for the years of lessons she learned from her that could not alone be captured in books.

A crackling sound struck her ears. A burning pain coursed through her back. Violet fell unto her knees steps away from the entrance. Her fist clinched as the hot burning pain rushed through her body. Stumbled and scrambled trying to get to her feet to turn around.

A Violet Night

Chapter 36.)

Another crackling sound filled the air clouded by the rumbling thunder overhead. Lighting flashed as more pain filled the side of her back. She fell on her hands and knees. "Face me!" Niran exclaimed over the fallen rain drops that were beginning to soften.

Violet grimaced with pain. She turned to face him slowly. "I have something for you. A gift if you would call it that." He said jumping off of his horse and reaching into the saddle bag. He smiled and tossed a hard object covered in cloth at her landing in the mud in front of her lap. She stared at it. He motioned her with his hands. She unwrapped the cloth slowly revealing one of Arrows paws. She dropped it and gasped "You're despicable!" She shouted. He smiled "You know this is how I love seeing you. On your knees looking at me in this way." He raised the whip once more. Violet closed her eyes tightly anticipating the pain to come.

He laughed "You're not even afraid of this are you?" His smile widened eagerly. He retracted his arm releasing to strike her in the shoulder. Violet let out a scream. He tossed the whip to the side of him "This was all just to get your attention. Don't you get it Violet? You make me do this to you. It's like you need me to do this to you.". He bent down and ran his fingers through her wet hair grabbing her face in his hands.

A flicker in his eyes changed. He slapped her across the face. She looked back up at him blood pouring from her mouth coating her teeth. Violet felt around with her tongue. She had bitten off a piece of her cheek. Niran yanked her off of the ground by her arms shoving her against the stone wall behind them. He grabbed her face with his hands once more. Violet was filled with rage. He traced her lips with his thumb smearing the blood across them slowly.

She spit in his face. He licked the blood off of his thumb with a silent laugh grabbing her by the shoulders he shoved her harder against the wall this time forcing her head to bang against it. She heard a loud ringing in her ears and the sound begin to fade when he did it a second time.

Her body slid down the smooth stone and into the mud below. "Get up!" He shouted at her still muffled through the ringing. She looked up at him. She was seeing two of him now. He continued shouting his voice sounded like he was deep underwater. She touched her head with her hand. There was a wet knot. She studied her hand over through the double vision. Blood covered her fingertips.

A Violet Night

He snatched her up by the wrist, grabbing her hair
and pulling her close so his lips were on her ear "Death is
too good for you." He whispered. She shoved his chest, but
her blows fell short everything was spinning around her.
She had no more energy to fight back. "*At least my baby is
safe.*" That thought alone brought her peace. She smiled to
herself.

"What are you smiling at?" He said gripping her
face tight. She placed her hand on top of his trying to pull
his fingers off. "My son will never have to grow from the
tainted ground in which his seed was left to rot in." She
said enraged. He loosened his grip on her "Where is my son
Violet?" He asked worried. She continued to smile at him.

"I will send out thousands of search parties for him,
and when he is returned home. I will teach him all of the
things that I know about women. That they're all only here
for a good fuck. That they're all useless and disposable like

his worthless mother.". "You're wrong. You will never find him." She said still smiling.

He shrugged his shoulders trying to control himself "And if we don't find him I suppose you'll be forced to have my children until you die Violet. There will never be a day where you won't have a piece of me inside of you, growing and moving around in your stomach.. After earlier I would not be surprised if there is already another one brewing deep inside your womb.". Violets smile faded as his grew "I watched you squirm underneath me. I heard all the sounds and breaths you took in my ear. I know you enjoyed yourself.".

He walked her back to the horse and tied the same thick rope around her wrist that she had on his and tightened it. He slapped it when he was done with the knot. "Expect this not to come off tonight." He said climbing back onto the horse looking at her in a tempted manner. The leaves rustled in front of them. "Ready to go on a run?" He asked raising his leg up to give the tall horse a kick.

"Niran!" Scarlets calm voice rang out in the wind. She stepped out from behind a tree. Violet looked up at her "No." She said weak. He looked at Violet and then at Scarlet. "Two birds with one stone I suppose. Only I have no use for you in my kingdom. I never did." He slid himself off of the horse. "This will be quick my dear." With a wink he smugly followed her back behind the brush and trees.

Violet pulled on the rope that was now tied down to the saddle. She grunted getting nowhere. She reached up to try and untie it but the sharp pain in her ribs prevented her from lifting her arms all the way up. "You can't hide from me little bird." He said pulling the bushes apart with his hands. Violet grabbed another hold of the rope and pulled with all of her might. Her wrist felt as if they would snap.

A Violet Night

She felt a hand wrap around her chest and one around her mouth. Violet froze. The black sleeved hand moved slowly from her mouth to his covered face. His gloved finger pressed against where his lips should be. His eyes, his eyes looked so faintly familiar. He pulled a knife out from behind his back. Her heart beat faster in her bruised chest. The man cut the rope in between her wrist effortlessly.

She looked up at the man. He turned his head quickly giving her a hard shove. She looked at him again. He shoved her harder motioning her to go. He turned and jogged after Scarlet and Niran. She waited a second and listened to the silence of the rain and wind before she ran stumbling on her own two feet. She opened the secret door closing it behind her she collapsed on the ground. She silently cried to herself. Her body was beyond sore.

"*Rowan.*" She thought as she stumbled back to her feet running down the hallway. She busted through the door and saw the sleeping baby on the bed. She sighed with relief and laid down next to him gently trying her best not to wake him up. She stroked his hair and pulled the blanket back over his little round shoulders. She closed her eyes with the sweet relief of his breathing mimicking her own. She smiled to herself kissing his head taking in his smell. It melted her into a wave of calmness.

A Violet Night

Chapter 37.)

"Scarlet!" Violet sat up in the bed. Her head was spinning. She stood up feeling the knot on her head again. Rowan rustled in the bed before facing the wall and falling back asleep. She peeked out of the window of the cottage and up at the clear night sky. She left the curtain pulled back letting the bright moonlight shine through on her face.

The hidden door began to move. Violet panicked, grabbing a candelabra from the table. Scarlet thrust herself through the door "Violet?" She shouted lowly. Violet dropped the heavy silver candelabra and hugged her sister tightly. "I thought you were dead." Violet whispered. "I could say the same about you." She giggled "Why are you just sitting in here in the dark?". She lit a few candles around the room. Violets eyes wondered with every flick of the dancing flames bouncing off of the walls. Scarlet turned around now in the light. Her face bruised and raised. Violet ran her fingers over Scarlets swollen eye. "I'm fine. I was but the distraction." She said grabbing her wrist and pulling it away. "I told you to have faith sister." She joked.

"Where is Niran?" She asked looking around the room again. Her eyes became fixated on the large shadow that had now invaded its way into the door frame. Scarlet began walking towards the door pulling the man out of the dark by his arm. He followed hesitantly. She stepped closer as Scarlet moved away. He froze. She nudged his shoulder from behind him with her hand.

The man grabbed at the cloth covering his face. Violet reached and met his hand with hers pulling it off slowly. It was as if time stood still. Rory in the flesh in front of her. The past few years were not kind to him. He looked tired and beaten down. He had gained width in muscle but lost the liveliness in his eyes. "Rory." She whispered covering her mouth as a thousand memories flooded into her mind.

He paused his movements again before dropping the mask and pulling her close to his chest. "I- thought you were-" Violet started to stutter. "I am here now." He whispered looking over her body to Scarlet who had weaved her way around them. "You know, I think I'm going to get some air." She said letting herself out of the front door.

"Where is Niran?" She repeated quietly pulling away from his embrace looking around him at the doorway. Rory's eyes hardened almost looking annoyed. He took her shoulders and set pushed her to the bed to sit. He stood above her and her son "Gone Violet. He's gone.". She pulled on his arm to sit beside her. He looked at the toddler in the bed and pulled his arm back to his body. Violet looked back at Rowan and then back at him. Her heart sunk in her chest. She knew why he didn't want to sit. He closed the entrance door trying to keep the draft out.

He pulled up a chair in front of her placing her knees in between his own. He brushed her cheek with his hand. She cupped his hand with hers against her face. She flashed a weak smile. He grabbed both of her hands in his own. "What do we do now?" She asked. "Now you rest." He said with no emotion. She looked at him confused how could he say that? How could he just tell her to go to sleep after the day she has had. After the years that she has endured. "No!" She said raising her voice at him. Rowan opened his eyes and sat up. "Yes. Violet." He said calmly looking at the boy staring back at him.

Rowan smiled at Rory. Violet stood up off the bed. "NO! Rory. You have been gone for so long." She said with a tremble in her voice. "Violet, stop before you scare your son. I am not going anywhere but outside for the night." He said calmly standing up.

The door creaked open as Scarlet let herself back in. "I-" Violet started to whisper. He shook his head and traded spots with Scarlet ushering her in the room. The door closed behind him swiftly.

Violet started towards the door after him. Scarlet grabbed her arm "Let him be Vi. This is hard on him too.". "Hard on him too?" She asked appalled ripping her arm away from her. "Violet. You don't know what hes done to be here. You don't understand what it must be like for him to see your son that you have with another man in front of him. A man that is capable of all the things he has done to you." She said looking at her tattered and broken down body. "I just need to talk to him." She said looking out the window at him as he sat in the grass looking up at the stars. "Tomorrow Vi." She whispered grabbing her around the shoulders pulling her back to the bed.

A Violet Night

Violet sat down her heart felt broken. After all these years he came back for her. So why did it feel like he had died all over again in an instant?

Her thoughts were interrupted by the sound of light running water as Scarlet wrung out a pale faded blue rag. She lightly cleaned her sisters face and wounds. Violet grimaced when she got to her back. She jerked away in pain.

"It needs to be done. You don't need an infection on top of everything else." She said sternly tossing the soiled dress into the corner of the room. "Here." She said pulling a huge men's night shirt from the small wooden dresser.

After getting most of the blood and mud out by brushing Violets hair Scarlet braided it letting it dangle down her spine. "How long has he been back?" She asked breaking the silence. Scarlet avoided the question with more silence. "How long?!" She asked again loudly. "I think these are questions for him to answer not me Vi.

Right now you need your rest." She said helping her sister

lay down. She laid beside her wrapping her arms around

her.

Violet knew the answer deep down in her stomach.

He has been back for a long while now. He just didn't want

to see her. She wondered to herself if Visha had been right

about him.

A Violet Night

Chapter 38.)

Scarlet cracked the door shut. She walked over to Rory "She's asleep.". Rory sighed in relief putting his arms behind his head and laying down in the grass. He looked up watching the stars twinkle above. "I know how hard this is for you Ri, but you have cut her a little slack." Scarlett said sitting on the ground next to him on her knees off to the side. "You don't get it." He said quietly. "Don't I?" She asked. "Do you know how hard it is to see that little boy? Do you know what it's like to hate a child you only just laid your eyes on?" He asked disgusted at his own thoughts.

"That little boy may have come from the worst person imaginable, but that little boy is the smartest, and brightest ray of sunshine I have EVER met in my life. His heart is so pure Ri. He maybe half of his father but he is also half of Violet too. Do not ever let yourself forget that. It has been so hard for her here these past few years without you and I am convinced that if Rowan wouldn't of came along there would be no Violet for you to come back for.". His posture shifted. He looked at her searching her eyes for more truths.

"I can't stop thinking about it." He said changing the subject. "I know. I was expecting much more of a fight from him." She said rubbing her swollen eye with her fingers. "He did get you pretty good." Rory joked. "You know he's not into fighting men.." She said still with a halfhearted joking tone. "So I have come to notice.." He said looking back at the cottage.

Images of him coming behind Niran as he attacked Scarlett over and over rushed through his head. He could still feel the pressure it took to puncture through his back with the sword. The release of weight as his body slid to the ground grabbing at Scarlets legs desperate for help. The gurgle sounds he made as he took his last breath. His last words on his tongue. "My sunshine." He had said painfully looking past Rory reaching with his hand.

Rory shook his head trying to forget. She patted his arm standing up "Do better Ri." She said hopeful walking back into the cottage. He nodded his head agreeing. He hadn't thought of it in that way. *"Tomorrow I will do better."* He thought to himself *"I have too."*.

His thoughts stiffened *"I need to get my mind off of this."* He stood up shaking his head and taking off his clothes down to his undergarments. He ran and jumped off of the rock into the water. The water was cold but refreshing as his head resurfaced above the water. He wiped the excess water from his eyes and squinted at Violet as she came towards the water's edge.

Violet met his gaze. She looked empty but whole at the same time. "I know you want your space, but have we not had enough distance between us?" She asked stepping her bare feet into the water. Rory stood up out of the water slowly walking towards her. "And I know things will never be exactly what they used to be.. I don't need them to be that way, but Ri I do need you in my life." Her eyes were filled with tears as she stepped closer letting the water splash just above her knees. She was now arm's length away from him, and all he wanted to do was kiss her.

"I just want to tell you-". Rory cut her off. "Violet, shut up." He said pulling her body to his own. He grabbed her waist in one hand careful not to grab her wounds and the back of her head with his fingers combed in her hair in another. He had missed her so much. His heart was beating out of his chest. She pulled apart from him. Her clothes clinging to his wet body and looked up into his eyes. Oh how he had missed her eyes. His smile faded into seriousness as he leaned down cautiously and kissed her again savoring the taste of her tongue on his.

All he could think about was ripping her clothes off of her body as she slid her hands up his torso and onto his jaw lines. She still after all this time knew how to make him feel vulnerable.

He placed his hands on her wrists and pulled them away. She looked at him angrily and placed them at the top of his neck as she began to kiss his more passionately. He gave in and kissed her aggressively. He picked her up carrying her to the soft grass. He laid her down straddling her hips below him. He brushed her loose hairs out of her face slowly. He smiled to himself. "What?" She asked gazing up at him. "Nothing, I am simply admiring your beauty".

A Violet Night

Rory looked at the cottage and then placed himself on the ground completely beside her. He held her hand pulling her closer. He could tell she wanted things to continue escalating, but it was more fun to make her want it.

She placed her head onto his chest listening to his heart beating, and watching his chest rise and fall with every breath. "Your son will be looking for you when the sun rises.". "Rowan. His name is Rowan." She said sitting up abruptly "He is but a child. You haven't even given him a chance, and yet I can already hear the disgust in your voice when you talk about him.". She shoved past him now standing above him "I was right.. Things are different, and I am glad you came when you did. But if these are your true colors, well... Then I don't need you anymore Rory ." She stormed off towards the cottage door.

Rory hadn't even realized what he had done, but that last part she said, *"Then I don't need you anymore."*

pierced his heart. He slapped both of his hands over his eyes "What's wrong with me? Rory do you even hear yourself speak?".

After all he had just seen the love of his life after all of this time apart. He felt her in his arms again. He knew he had to make this right with her. He knew he had to give Rowan a fair chance. Scarlet was right. This little boy is still apart of Violet. A huge piece of her heart walking this earth beside her. He was no longer the only man in her life that she loved, and in that moment he realized he would never come first in her life again. "I will make this right." He said to himself throwing a stick into the water watching the ripples grow. "I will make this right.".

The mosquitoes nibbled at his arms and legs. He swotted at them slipping back into his clothes tossing his soaking wet undergarments to the side. He stood up gathering sticks from by the cottage and chopped wood he had placed safely out of the rains view.

A Violet Night

He picked a grassy spot near the water and started a fire in hopes to dry the rest of his clothes and keep the bugs off of him for the night. He brought his knees to his chest crossing his arms overtop feeling the heat on his skin from the flames. He yawned and laid down on his stomach falling asleep watching the flames dance together.

"Wake up Moron. We have things to do." Scarlet said splashing water on the bed of ashes. Rory opened his eyes. The sun had not begun to rise yet. He shivered sitting up putting his hand in the dew covered grass.

"Feeling frisky are we?" She asked pointing to his underpants laying on the ground. He opened his mouth. She put her hand up "I don't want to know.". He laughed at her.

"She asked how long you have been back last night." She said holding her hand out to help him up. "What did you tell her?" He asked nervously extending his arm. "That she needs to talk to you about it." She said truthful.

"What should I tell her?" He asked. "The truth Rory. She deserves to know the truth and nothing less." Scarlet said picking up his underpants with a stick to fling at him. He caught them in the air "What do I say. Oh hey. I came back while you were pregnant thought you were having a better life then you let on and then lived in hiding until now?".

"That would be the truth now wouldn't it." She looked at him seriously "The words will come to you in the moment.". She punched him in the shoulder walking ahead of him. "I hope so." He said catching up to her pace. Rory hesitated reaching for the doorknob on the cottage door.

A Violet Night

Chapter 39.)

Violet closed the door softly and peeked out at Rory still sitting on the grass from the window. She breathed heavily closing the curtains and laying back down on the bed. She could feel her eyelids closing but her mind was still racing.

She awoke from her dream drenched in sweat. She was having flashbacks from the day before. Flashes of Nirans face still fresh in her mind, Arrow's paw laying on the ground, Elda's lifeless body lying on that cold floor, and Rory's stiff face emerging from the darkness.

A Violet Night

"Hungry mommy." Rowan said shaking her arm. She grabbed on to the bed for support to pull her aching body up. Scarlet wasn't in the room. She opened the door... Rory was also gone.

"Mommmmmmyyyy." Rowan cried. She then remembered the supplies were in the cabinet. She opened a cabinet door folded neatly inside was her white slip she traced the lace with her fingers. She smiled remembering how that day felt. She closed the door opening another until she unraveled a cloth and pulled a piece of bread out from dinner last night. The overpowering smell instantly made her think of Elda. She shook her head and turned around giving it to her son. He scarfed it down.

She knew he would soon be thirsty as well. Violet grabbed a glass pitcher from off the table and went out and fetched some water for the day. *"They'll be back soon."* She told herself, but after a day filled with running around in the grass chasing Rowan and reading almost all of the books off the shelf of the cottage to him she had begun to worry.

She began to rethink her situation and where they could have gone off too, or if it had all been a dream dreamt up by her tormented damaged mind.

The end of the day came quickly. She lit the fireplace in the corner of the room walking to the bed and laid down next to Rowan humming to him stroking his hair until he fell asleep. She tucked him in with a kiss sitting herself up careful not to wake him.

The stone entrance door began to jiggle. Rory, and Scarlet entered the room. "Why did you leave me here?" She whispered loudly. "You needed your rest, and you cannot be spotted right now." Scarlet said sitting at the small table. "You should have woken me up!" Violet said crossing her arms. "Shut up and stop throwing a fit." Rory said sitting down next to Scarlet. He was wearing the guard uniform with the mask hanging from his belt. Her heart began to race again suddenly realizing in this light that he had been under her nose all of these years.. "You can't be seen right now Vi." Scarlet restated.

"How long?" She whispered bitterly pointing to the mask. Without a skip of a beat he responded. "Only once.. You seemed happy when you spoke to me." He took a breath "So I let you be.". "Happy?" She asked replaying the exact moment he was talking about.

The pieces all finally fit together for her "You could have saved me! You could have saved all of us! Elda would still be alive if you had!".

"People make mistakes Vi. He's only human. You played your part to the staff and public very well. How was he to know?" Scarlet said I his defense. Violet sighed not wanting her to be right. "I spent the day holding a search party for you." Scarlet said changing the subject before

Violet could erupt again "Everyone thinks you, Niran and Rowan were kidnapped for ransom. Elda was but a mistaken casualty and I got the back end of the fight.". "I even wrote a ransom note for them to find." Rory said smugly.

"Where do we go from here?" Violet asked sitting down with them cutting eyes at Rory. "A week from yesterday guards will find you bound and stumbling back to the castle with Rowan. You will tell them you escaped your captor, and that Niran is dead. If they ask what happened you will tell them it was to horrific and gruesome. You will cry pitifully." Rory said leaning over his lap and grabbing her hands in his.

Violets face became flushed with heat. She pulled away still angry that he left her with that monster. She couldn't help but stare into his eyes. Her eyes dropped to his mouth watching his lips turn into a grin. She pulled down on the large shirt she still had on wiggling it to the center of her thighs again. He watched her carefully with his gaze.

"In all seriousness you are going to have to sell your performance Vi." Scarlet said realizing what was happening and standing up to crawl into the bed with Rowan.

"Oh, Arrow will be okay by the way. I cleaned her wounds. She will heal as long as she doesn't fester." She said covering up and snuggling up to the toddlers little body. Violet's heart instantly lifted at the thought of Arrow safe.

"I brought this back for you." Rory said reaching into his satchel. He pulled out a spare dress for Violet, a matching ribbon for her hair, soaps a mirror and her hairbrush. She smiled at him even though the sight of the hairbrush made her sick. But how was he to know where it had come from. He reached into the bag once more and pulled out a small heavily worn shirt and pants for Rowan along with a small wooden dog.

"I made this of Arrow while at war. It was for you but now want him to have it." Rory said placing it in her hands with a tender smile. Violets heart skipped a beat. She leaned in and kissed his cheek. "Thank you" She whispered to him appreciably. He nodded his head. She broke eye contact with him not knowing what else to say.

"I suppose I should go get cleaned up then." She said gathering her things from the table and heading to the door awkwardly stumbling into the frame pulling down on the shirt again. He nodded his head at her crossing his arms.

"You could come out there with me you know." She said softly fumbling and dropping her soap. He grinned at her amused now standing. He squatted down by her feet looking up at her with his devilish grin. Rory came close to her standing up again and placing her soap on top of her pile. He placed one hand above her on the top of the door frame and moved his other hand past her waist before opening the door for her.

"I think I will let you have your privacy." He said looking down at her. She rolled her eyes "Suit yourself." She said. "Yuck." Scarlet said from the bed. They ignored her.

Violet looked at his eyes, and then to his jaw. He clenched it harder making his muscle twitch. "Excuse me Mr. Guerrero." She whispered to him with a warm smile. He let out a playful graveled laugh watching her tur to walk away.

A Violet Night

Chapter 40.)

Rory paused a moment before pulling open the curtain. He stood and watched as Violet slowly slipped off her clothes. She looked back over her shoulder at the cottage. He closed the curtain, but there was no doubt in his mind that she had seen him watching her.

He gulped feeling his face become flushed, "*What am I doing? This isn't the first time I've seen her in this way. So why do I feel like this?*".

"Just go out there already." Scarlet said annoyed with her eyes closed "You and I both know you are going to so why has it taken you this long.".

A Violet Night

Before he realized what he was doing he had already opened the door and was walking outside. He closed the door quietly making sure not to wake up the boy.

Rory watched her go under the water and come back up facing the waterfall as she lathered her body with the soap.

He approached. Violet was leaning back in the water washing her hair. The closer he got to her the more he could make out every glistening bead of dripping water off of her skin. "Are you getting in, or are you just going to watch?" She said not turning to look at him. Rory slowly as if in a trance removed his clothes and got into the water.

His body shivered. The water was so much colder than the night before. He splashed some water on his chest and arms. Goosebumps overwhelmed his body. He came within a few feet from her.

A Violet Night

Violet turned towards him with a smile almost too eager to see him. His mouth cracked opened a little bit looking at her face and her wet hair *"She is so beautiful."*. His eyes wondered to her chest. He noticed the scars. She tensed up submerging herself more into the water.

Rory came closer to her lifting her up out of the depths. Moving her hair he traced her scars with his thumbs "I am sorry I was not there for you when you needed me the most.". He embraced her pressing her wet skin to his own. He kissed her hair "I shouldn't have left you Violet. I should have fought it. We could have ran.".

She pushed her hands against his chest looking up at him "No.. If we would have run they would only have found us. Then we'd both be dead, and I wouldn't have that sweet little boy in there." She paused "Please don't pity me. In a way.. The day you left I did too. I was no longer the keeper of my own body, and all I had left was my mind; although even in time I no longer owned that either... Ri, I-am no longer the same person I was when you left me. I am his mother before anything else now. And beyond that I am unsure how to be anything else to anyone.".

He held her face in his hand prompting her to look up at him. His thumbs digging into her jaw. He kissed her. Her mouth tasted sweet as their tongues swirled together almost as if in a dance. He pulled away "Then let me make you feel alive again.". She looked up at him excitedly and curious.

He continued kissing her picking her up in the water careful not to touch her wounded upper back. She wrapped her legs around his body. He struggled to walk through the mud sticking to his feet in the water. She kissed and sucked on his neck while they broke the shoreline. He laid her down in the grass slightly out of view of the cottage window.

A Violet Night

He grabbed her hips pulling her into position entering her. He bit his lip. "Fuck" He whispered. She was beyond the wettest she had ever been for him "I have missed you.".

Just as he had begun to pleasure her she pushed on his shoulders panicking to get off of her. He cupped the side of her face in his hand "I'm not him Violet. We can stop if I am hurting you.". She looked at him lovingly "I have missed you every single day, and I am yet to stop loving you." She said pulling him farther inside of her.

"I have never stopped loving you Violet." He whispered back into her ear. He felt her goosebumps on her arms while she wrapped them tightly around his neck.

He finished on her. He felt her whole-body shake letting out a loud moan arching her back in his arms. He held her for a second before kissing her on the forehead. He laid on the ground next to her listening to each other's heavy panting. There were no words to say. In this moment everything in Rory's life felt complete.

She scooted herself over and laid her head on his chest. "If we stay right here I will fall asleep, and I don't think this is the sight Scarlet wants to see." He chuckled kissing her head again and picking a blade of grass out of her hair. She lifted her head up and kissed his lips softly.

"Shall we do what we came out here to do now?" She said standing up with a grin. He sat up admiring her new physical shape. She had stretchmarks on her stomach, thighs, and butt. Something he had never found attractive before was suddenly one of his biggest turn ons with her. He smacked her on the ass, biting his lip as it jiggled. "I guess we can do that." He said smiling at her glare of excitement she turned and raced back into the water. He ran after her chasing her like he had done all those years ago. Catching up to her he grabbed her around the waist swinging her around laughing.

Together they bathed each other taking breaks only to hold one another in the water. "Rory?" She asked hugging his arms letting her body float. "Hmm?" He swooped her around to face him. "Why didn't you take your mask off when you saw me?" She asked sounding disappointed. He let out a sigh "When Niran and Visha came to the camp he made it seem as if you had moved on with him. I didn't fully believe him of course but watching you both interact in that hall I overreacted. I have been right here ever since. Hoping one day that you would return to visit this place and I could surprise you.".

"So all of those acquired things inside? Those are all from you?" She asked looking up at him. He nodded "I do have quite the junk collection going for me don't I?" He laughed nervously.

"I was here. Right after I had Rowan.". He nodded again "I figured it had been you moving my things around.". "Where were you then?" She asked worried that he might have seen her with her intrusive thoughts. "With my uncle in his room trying to get the latest scoop on Lee. Violet.. I truly am sorry for how everything happened to you. It wasn't fair." He said looking lost into her eyes. She searched his face "You're here now.. That's all that matters Ri." She said giving him a long hug. He squeezed her tight.

"Oh, I loved the way you carved your name. Your penmanship my love was impeccable given the canvas." He said pulling her slightly away. "I know it was over kill right?" She joked. "I think he deserved way more for what he has put you through." He said with a dry laugh. "Let's dry off the sun will be rising in a short few hours." She said rubbing his arm.

A Violet Night

Chapter 41.)

"Shhhh.." Violet hushed Rory giggling as she opened the creaking door. "If you are finished with whatever that was out there." Scarlet paused heading to the tunnel door. "Did you have a nice nap?" He asked gleefully. "I have had better. There were some odd animal noises outside… but I need to be getting back before they miss me.". Rory and her exchanged concerning looks before he waved her on with his devilish smile. She shook her head closing the door behind her.

Rory turned back to Violet "And you should be getting some rest as well my lady.". Violet agreed in her head. He had worn her out. He watched her crawl into the bed next to her son scooting him over with her arm as she went. Rory sat down on the floor beside the bed. "What are you doing?" Violet asked almost sounding offended. She proceeded to open up the covers and pat the spot next to her.

He hesitantly looked at her and the boy. "Well come on or don't." She said dropping the covers and turning towards Rowan. He watched as she placed her hand on his little head.

Rory held his breath placing his body next to hers wrapping his arm around her waist. He had forgotten how their bodies fit like a glove together. It sent comfort in his heart that she was next to him again in his arms.

Rory felt a soft little hand wrap around his own. He couldn't help himself as uncomfortable as he felt in that moment he sighed with relief that lifted his heart in a sense.

A Violet Night

He felt his eyes begin to get heavy and for the first time in a long time he felt as if he was home. There was something about the way she tried to match his breathing that made him smile like a child.

Rory awoke from the best sleep he had had in a long while. He peeked over Violets sleeping body she was now facing him her head just below his chin. The boy was no longer in his place. He looked out the window above the foot of the bed. The sun had barely risen. Rory wiped the sleep from his eyes, and slowly turned around in the bed placing his feet firmly on the floor.

He looked up to the sound of soft rustling. Rowan was standing on a chair trying to unwrap the left out bread. Careful not to wake her up Rory stood up covering Violet with the blanket to her shoulders. He noticed the boy tense up and begin to look as if he was in trouble. Rory placed his finger to his lips and whispered to him "Shhh. Mommy's sleeping." Pointing to Violet he let out a smile reaching past him to break a piece off for him. Rowan placed both hands covering his mouth and let out a quiet laugh. Rory handed it to him pulling up a chair next to him and patting his head softly.

Rowan climbed from his chair to Rory's nestling himself into his lap dropping crumbs everywhere. Scarlets voice rang through his head *"He's half of Violet too."* He wrapped his arms around the boy placing his chin on his head. "I will never let anyone hurt you." He whispered to him. To which Rowan smiled big and offered him a piece of bread he had drenched in his saliva. "Oh yummy." He replied laughing and pretending to eat it. Rowan giggled loudly waking up his mother. Rory became worried. He was suddenly unsure if he should remain sitting with the boy on his lap or if he should put him down.

She opened her eyes and smiled at them. "So you're not going to share with your own mother? How rude!" She said jokingly "Gone." He said raising his little hands above his head. "Go back to sleep. I can watch him." Rory said standing up with the toddler in his arms. She smiled at him. He leaned down and kissed her nose. Rowan copied him with a smile.

Violet smiled lovingly at the two of them. She rolled back over. Quietly with Rowan still in arm he picked up the space around him making oats on the fire, sweeping, and moving around the clutter. He sat Rowen down and fed him a bowl of oats he had dowsed in ground cinnamon and sugar. Putting their dishes away he noticed the boy rubbing his eyes and letting out a large yawn.

"Alright kid." He said poking the embers left on the dull fire. He wiped the crumbs from his small rosy cheeks with his hand. Rowan leaned his forehead to Rory's. He placed his hand on his back with his opposite hand.

A Violet Night

Rory let out a smile and laid him back down beside his mother. He nestled up next to her scooting himself under the blanket.

He sat back in the chair crossing his arms and legs stretching them out. He watched them sleep peacefully from across the small room. He scoffed to himself never did he imagine this is how his life would go.

Rory had never put much thought into living past 20 let alone to be 27. He had more than he ever dreamed he would, the girl, and now her son.

"No please stop.!" Violet said in her sleep thrashing her arms up. He went to her lying next to her for comfort. He gave her a squeeze. Her green eyes opened dilating fully "Oh Rory I thought this was all a dream. I thought you were gone again.". "I am never leaving you again Violet. That I can promise you both." He said looking at

Rowan. She rubbed the bridge of his little nose with her thumb.

"Can we stay here with you forever?" She asked. He smiled "Maybe someday but for now we need to worry about getting you home without raising anymore concerns." He said laying his head on hers. "It was a stupid question I am sorry." She said. "Do not apologize to me. No one called your question stupid." He said annoyed his face softened "We just have things we need to do before we disappear.".

She smiled to herself "Can we have chickens?" She asked amused. "Chickens?" He asked. "Mmhmm. Chickens." She said again. He let out a laugh "We can have whatever your heart desires.".

A Violet Night

Chapter 42.)

"It has to look fresh.. Are you ready?" Rory said hesitantly. "Do it. This will be nothing compared to what I am used too." Violet said becoming tense. She gripped her knees tightly together with her hands tucked firmly in between.

Rory raised his hand up and with hesitation he slapped her across the face. He grabbed her immediately afterward. She looked up at him. His handprint almost covered the entire side of her face. She pushed herself off of him and began to put on her dress from her final encounter with Niran. He watched her slide it on over her scabbed and tender back. He couldn't even begin to imagine what that must have felt like for her.

She grabbed a fist full of the dress in her hands looking at the dried blood splatters, mud stains, and torn edges. Ri gently grabbed her hands and gently made her release her grip to tell her "Everything is going to be okay.". She weakly smiled at the ground.

"Stop worrying so much. You'll do fine. Everyone is in such a panic trying to find you that they will believe anything you say at this point." He kissed her head giving her a hug from behind. "Just remember when this hourglass empties wrap him up, hold him tight and run. Don't stop, go straight through the woods towards the castle walls. Not the road. Not the gate. The wall by the garden. You scream, and cry let all of your tears flow. Put on a show as soon as you see the search party stay hidden if you are too early. Avoid all questions about Niran. Scarlet and I will take care of that once his body has been discovered.".

A Violet Night

She grabbed her napping child off the bed. He walked to the table and picked up the palm sized hourglass. "Wait." She said nervously looking up from Rowan. He took another hourglass out of his pocket and flipped them both simultaneously. "There is no more time for waiting my love." He said giving her a wink and heading out of the passageway. He closed the door behind him and took a deep breath. He was beyond nervous, but he could never let her see that.

Walking back to the road to not look suspicious he passed a young mother with her twin toddler girls in her arms. He smiled at them. They were fighting over two dolls. The more thinned out girl dropped them both out of anger.

Rory leaned down beside the trio picking the dolls up for her. She smiled at him while he dusted it off. "Thank you." The women said appreciative. "No problem." He said looking at the dolls in his hands playfully pulling them out of the girls reach to make them giggle. "They're beautiful." He said to the woman who jumped up a little to push them farther on her hips. "They are definitely a handful that is for sure." She joked.

He knew he had to hurry he had no time to delay. He nodded reaching in his pocket and slipping her some coins into her side bag hanging off her shoulder. "No I can't." She said. "Too late I'm already walking away, and your hands are far too full to chase me down." The women smiled at him "Thank you again for your kindness sir.". He nodded at her and continued on his way.

He made his way back to the castle making sure to put his masked hood over his face before entering and finding his way to Scarlet. She glanced at him rubbing her hand across her cheek twice. He checked the hourglass in his pocket. Only a few beads of sand remained. He nodded his head at her remaining silent.

A Violet Night

His attention drew to Harriet who was biting her nails . Scarlet nudged her shoulder. "We must bring the royal family home at once!" Harriet said pulling herself together. Lee helped her stand up. She patted his arm tenderly "I must know what has become of them…". "You heard her men, get moving. There is no time left to waste!" Scarlet shouted at the captains, commanders, and higher up knights in the room.

Rory and the others nodded their heads and quickly left the room. He listened to them chatter on about their theories walking amongst themselves to exit the room.

The men formed into 3 large groups. The first and the largest led by his uncle was to stay at the Castle with Harriet in case someone where to try another 'kidnapping'. Meanwhile the other two fell into the search parties on the grounds.

A Violet Night

Group one is where Lee 'happened' to fall. Rory wanted to make sure Violet and Rowan were found fairly quickly. Not immediately but still by someone he trusted.

The groups began to march onward towards the main road. From there the two parties where split into two more groups now becoming four smaller equally sectioned off amounts. They took off one group per each direction. One going East and the other going West and so forth. Rory made sure he fell into the West group of searchers to find Nirans corpse.

They began into the woods. After what felt hours of looking for the smallest things he heard and frantic "Over here!". A couple hundred yards from the Garden resided Nirans body. Leaves sticking to his now bloated skin. The smell was more pungent in the sunlight then last night when Scarlet and he had dumped it.

A Violet Night

The two whom found him began to vomit violently.
"Roll him up." A knight said tossing a large blanket at
Rory and another man. As they moved his body his flesh
wounds became more visual exposing the maggots eating
away at him. Flies and gnats swarmed the air around them.
Rory pulled his shirt over mask and his nose taking in a
deep breath of clean air from over his shoulder. The other
man began dry heaving. "*Pussy*" he thought to himself.

He laid the large deep purple velvet blanket out in
front of him. Together, Rory at the feet and the other man
at his shoulders rolled him over on top of it. From there
using the blanket to roll him up with.

Rory looked at the piece of the back of Nirans scalp
dangling from his rotting flesh with the final roll to cover
him. His insides shook thinking about the sound his head
had made bouncing off the chest when Scarlet accidentally
dropped her end trying to pull him out. They loaded his

body onto a horse tying it down and another guard took it body back to the castle.

Just then he heard it. He heard Violet Screaming her loudest. Everyone looked around with large, startled eyes at one another. They began to run to the sound of her screams. Rory made sure to stay in the back of the group watching from a distance.

"Someone! Anyone. Help me please!" Violet screamed at the top of her lungs. Once she saw the group she tripped over her own feet clutching her son in her arms. Rowan was crying confused.

"My Queen!" The men all began to try and help her at once. Rory and Violet made eye contact even through his mask. Her face was red and swollen from the salty tears gushing down her cheeks. She had ratted up her hair and splashed more dirt and mud on herself and her son.

"What happened?". "What happened to you?" Some of the men asked. Lee swooped her and Rowan up in an embrace forcing them onto another horse immediately that rode back to the castle with no haste. Rory let out an internal sigh of relief. It was finally over.

The men began to cheer, hugging themselves and high fiving loudly. A man accidently bumped into Rory. "Bastard got what was coming to him eh." He said with a cocky smile. Rory envisioned the imprint on the ground from Nirans rotting grey corpse. "Sure did." Another man said spitting on the ground. "No doubt in my mind he is covered in brimstone right about now." He joked to Rory. "Drinks on me at the tavern tonight men!" One of the knights shouted looking around as if he alone had solved this mystery. They all shouted again slapping each other on the back.

A Violet Night

Chapter 43.)

"Oh cousin!" Harriet exclaimed rushing to hug

them. She grabbed Violets shoulders looking her over "You

poor thing.." She whispered hugging her a second time.

"Daddy!" Rowen shouted pointing to the halls of the castle.

Harriet's tears flowed from her face. Violet pulled his little

body closer to her chest. His words stung in her heart.

"Violet he has been murdered!" She wept harder. "I

know." Violet said hushed grabbing her sons soft head.

"You had to watch?!" She asked loudly more upset.

Thinking on her feet she said "No-no. I only heard the

sounds.. I never saw the attackers faces. Their accents

where too thick for me to understand what they were saying to him.". "Must have been the Eastern Kingdom. Such cowards." She scolded hatefully "It is just a little too convenient that the week surrounding your kidnapping they 'surrendered' their battles.".

She sighed with relief knowing she suspected nothing. "Come now let us go get you bathed." She said looking at her knotted up hair. Violet turned around looking for Rory. There were so many men in guard uniforms that she could not pick him out. "You are safe now." Harriet reassured her. "Safe at last." Violet whispered with a smile.

She opened the doors to their chamber. Violet looked around at them room. Not a thing was out of place from that night. She set Rowan on the floor. He ran to his corner and began to play with his toys. Violet looked at the table of Nirans scribbled notes. She thumbed through the stack. Until she found a folded one addressed to her. She looked astonished picking it up and tucking it into the lining of her dress.

"Your water is ready." Scarlet said coming out of the privy drying her hands off on a towel. She shared a smile with her. She dropped her dress on the floor carefully hiding the note underneath the clean towels. She sat in the warm bath water letting it run over her body. Scarlet plopped Rowen's naked body in Violets lap. Harriet handed him his carefully crafted bath boats to play with. They began setting soaps and calming elixirs next to the tub. "I think, if it is okay I would like to bathe on my own." She said blowing bubbles at her son from her cupped hands.

They nodded sweetly at her and left the room. She hummed to herself as she lathered up Rowen and herself watching him giggle every time she poured water over his head.

A Violet Night

She sat him on the counter draped in the big fuzzy hooded towel still fidgeting with his toy in hand. Wrapping herself up she pulled out the note. She held it in her hands folding it over and over unsure what she wanted to do with it. "Vi." Scarlets voice startled her. She peeked over her shoulder to see if she was alone. She was.

"Are you going to read it?" She asked. "I saw it on the table when I came in that's why it was almost at the bottom of the pile." She said rubbing Rowen down with the towel. "No.. I don't think that I want to know what it says." She said crumpling the paper in her hands. "Set it over there and I will burn it for you." Scarlet said taking it from her. Harriet come inside the room hairbrush in hand "Are you ready to tackle this mess?" She asked pulling Violet to a chair.

Scarlet walked to the fireplace moving it around with the prodder. She reached into her pocket. She paused thinking about what if Violet wanted the note one day. She took it out of the envelope and tossed the envelope in the

open fire. She looked at Violet then grabbed Rowen off the

counter to get him ready.

That night a feast was made in the honor of the

fallen king. Along with the safe return of Violet and

Rowan. Rory looked across the ball room making eye

contact with Violet. She was making conversation with

higher ups. He watched her hands fly around as she spoke

wildly. She was smiling widely at his uncle who brought

her in for a hug. He admired that when she talked

passionately her hands took on a life of their own. Rowan

was running around her feet chasing Arrow. Who hobbled

around barking with joy.

A flash of memories overwhelmed his head and

heart of the first time they were in here together. He

remembered every small detail about her including her

scent from that night. The way the moon reflected on her

hair. He smiled at her before subsuming to his own thoughts.

"Thoughts? Emotions?" Scarlet asked popping up out of nowhere next to him. She turned her attention to her sister as well. "So what now? Everything just goes back to the way it was before I left?" He asked with a saddening tone. Scarlet took a sip of her drink before handing it to Rory. He pushed it back to her. "God I hope not." She said with a laugh. He pushed her arm in light of her joke. "I think I just need some air." He said to her placing his hand on her shoulder. "Don't disappear for too long now." She said taking another big drink.

"Excuse me I was wondering what-" Harriet said tapping Rory on the shoulder. He turned around already annoyed. She took a step back in the hallway. "You're supposed to be dead." She gasped. "I am dead." He said blankly. She pushed his shoulder with her palm cautiously stepping back again as Rory jumped at her. She hit him again turning her shock into frustration "Does she know?"

She asked concerned. "Know what? I am but a free spirit."

He said walking away from her. "Rory! Does she know?"

She shouted to him. "Who is Rory?" He asked trying to

contain his laughter. She grunted loudly reentering the

ballroom.

He roamed the halls retracing his memories he had

once made with her all those long nights ago. He found

himself making his way back to the bench they first shared

together. He sat there looking out over the skyline. The

stars twinkled and danced above him. The moon was at its

fullest for the month illuminating everything below the

balcony. Everything around him looked as it did that night

they shared together.

"Is this seat taken?" Violets voice rang out in his

ears like the feel of the softest silk in someone's hands. He

felt her hands on his shoulder. He looked around behind her

to make sure no one was watching. He grabbed her hand

with his right hand. She sat next to him resting her head on his shoulder. "You don't have to look over your shoulder anymore Ri. There is no longer anyone above me.". "Rowan?" He whispered kissing her on the forehead. "With Scarlet dancing his little heart out." She said. He smiled at the thought of him with his drunken aunt "I love you Violet.". "I love you more Rory.". "Most." She said. "Forever." He answered . "Always... I Promise." She finished. He rubbed her face in his hands and kissed her again.

Together they sat watching the night. It was their night together again at long last. Rory smiled to himself, after all this time he had his own perfect *"Violet night."*.

A Violet Night

Chapter 44.) *Epilogue*

"Lilliana!" Violet shouted out of the door of the cottage. A small skinny girl with golden brown eyes and freckles ran to the door. "Yes momma?" She asked. "Tell your brother to stop playing about and wash up we are going to see Aunt Scarlet today." She said looking at her daughters frizzed hair. Her eyes lit up. "Yay!" She yelled in excitement racing out the door.

"Rowan! Mom said to get your dirty, stinky butt up here now!" She screamed while running to her brother. Her long braided hair slapping her on the back as she went. Arrow racing at her side.

A Violet Night

Rory stopped skinning the rabbit he had been working on laughed looking at Violet pointing his knife at her "I don't know where she got that from right?". Violet looked at him smugly and shoved his chest.

"Rowan, Lilliana. Let's go!" She shouted. The children came running Arrow racing just ahead of them now with her tongue wildly out to the side. She kissed both of her kids on the head and headed inside. Violet looked at Arrow panting hard. Her snout now white and grey from age. She pet her on the head while she flopped over.

"Do we have to get all dressed up again?" Rowan asked washing his face and hands off with a damp rag. Violet nodded and pointed towards the hallway leading to the kids newly added bedrooms. There once crammed cottage for two was now transformed into a 3 bedroom cottage to fit their newly growing family.

A Violet Night

Violet looked outside at Rory. He finished up what he was doing tossing his tools into the shack that also housed their half a dozen chickens. Well a half dozen on a good day. Arrow liked to sneak herself a chicken every now and again. He threw grain on the ground for the mas he shut them inside.

"I don't know why you're so worried about the time Vi. You know she has never been one to complain about us being late." He said cleaning off with the used rag on the table. She picked it up disgusted that it reeked of animal fat tossing it in the clothes basket to be washed.

This time was different. Scarlet wanted to introduce them to 'the love of her life' as she had put it. "Here mommy." Lilliana said handing a hairbrush to her mom. Violet undid her braid letting her long curly hair flow to the middle of her back. She brushed it out and pulled it back with a long red ribbon leaving just a few strands of hair down by her ears.

A Violet Night

"Do I look pretty daddy?" She asked twirling around in her fancy dress. Rory swooped her up in his arms "Pretty? Where? All I see is two of the most beautiful girls I've ever laid my eyes upon." He said giving Violet a kiss. "Yeah, pretty ugly." Rowan said jokingly tucking in his shirt. Liliana scrunched up her nose at him and stuck out her tongue "You're just mad dad didn't call you beautiful!". "Yeah.. that's right." Rowan said rolling his eyes. Rory rustled Rowan hair aggressively "Do you want me to call you beautiful too son?". "Daaaaad." Rowan said pushing his hand off with a smile.

Violet laughed "Alright, alright.". The entrance way began to open. Lee stepped inside. "Uncle Lee!" The kids ran to him giving him a hug. He half squatted and embraced the little arms "Ready?" He said getting in position to race the kids through the passageway. "Go!" He shouted taking off ahead of them. "No fair!" Lilliana shouted. "Yeah cheater! Your legs are longer than ours." Rowan said letting his sister go through first.

"You have everything?" Rory asked Violet. "We're just staying a couple of days." She said looking over the two big bags on the table "I think we packed more than enough this time.".

"Can I lead?" Rowan asked sitting at the front of the carriage with Lee. "I don't see why not." He said slipping the rains to Rowan. "Everyone on?" Lee asked looking behind him. Lilliana sat on Rory's lap. "How come I can't lead?" She asked stubbornly crossing her arms "Rowan always gets to do everything!". "When you're a little bigger I'll teach you too." Lee said smiling at her. "Well I guess that's okay then. It gives me more time to work on more important things." She said smiling back at him.

Lee put his hands behind his head leaning against the seats cushion. "Easy does it." He said to Rowan who slapped the reigns gently. Lee placed his hat over his eyes and leaned back farther to stretch out crossing his arms.

Rowen hit a bump in the road interrupting Lee's snooze. He jumped up his hat nearly flying away. Lilliana laughed loudly from behind making her brother giggle as well.

"How was the ride over?" Scarlet asked reaching up for Lilliana. "It was so bumpy Aunt Scarlet. Rowan thinks he's a good leader, but he really isn't yet." She said wrapping her arms around her neck and hopping down.

"Shut up! Like you could do any better!" He said jumping down and giving his aunt a hug. "Probably could have." She mumbled to her brother. Violet rolled her eyes at the children. "So where is he?" Violet said greeting Scarlet with a kiss on each cheek and a hug. "How very cutthroat and straight to the point today aren't we sister."

She said with a laugh "Let's get you settled, and you'll meet at dinner tonight.". Violet looked at her stubbornly.

"Mommy can we go play?" Liliana asked tugging on her mother's dress. She nodded her head "Yes, go but stay with your brother.". With that the children took off into the castle. Arrow jumped down from the carriage and stretched out her back. "Hiya sweet girl!" Scarlet said crouching down to love on the dog. "I got your paw." She said grabbing her nub. "Oh that is just wrong." Rory said with a laugh. "I see Vi has learned to cook, or are you expecting number three?" She asked smacking him in the stomach. Rory put her in a headlock. "Is this any way to treat your queen?" She asked through his arm. He released her. "Don't get me for treason now." He joked. "If you do not watch yourself I just might." She said fixing her blouse.

"I will help you take your bags up." Lee said grabbing at the two bags. Rory grabbed them from him and asked, "What are you doing?". Lee looked at him confused.

"But I'll tell you what. You can walk with me while I put these away and then we can go and catch up.". Rory said walking ahead of him. He caught up to his friend and took one of the bags from his shoulder to lighten his load.

Violet followed them upstairs to her old room. She ran her fingers across the thick silk sheets. "Do you ever miss it?" Scarlet asked from behind her. Violet nodded "Sometimes.". "You know you can always come back. There is more than enough room for all of you here. Also it just doesn't seem right to have all of this without the one who gave it to you by your side. Even if it is only until my nephew comes of age." Scarlet said walking to her. "You know this place.. it never made me happy." Violet said. Scarlet looked at her and squinted her eyes sarcastically "I'll let you get freshened up before dinner.". "Stay!" Violet said. "I mustn't.. buuuuut okay!" She said tackling her sister on the bed. They laughed like children arm in arm.

A Violet Night

"So tell me more about 'The love of your life!"
Violet said excitedly rolling onto her belly "You have only
kept them a secret for a whole year you know.". "Oh you're
in for a surprise that's for sure." She said with a smile.
"Dear sister I do believe you are blushing!" She said
teasing her. "I will not say another word!" Scarlet said
hitting her sister in the head with a pillow.

"You're killing me! Absolute torture!" She shouted
dramatically throwing it back at her. She caught it and set it
in her lap. "You have endured much worse torture then this,
so I am sure this you will survive." She said raising an
eyebrow at her.

The sound of children's screaming and laughing
filled the air. They walked to the balcony watching the
Rowen and Lilliana run around with two dark haired girls a
little taller than Rowen. Climbing and jumping out of a tree
at each other. Violet smiled and laughed. Scarlet looked

over the edge with an uneasy look. She fixed her face

quickly.

"Who's darling girls are these?" She asked

watching them play together. "A maids." She said fast.

Violet looked at her "Well I think it is very kind of you to

allow them inside the walls while their mother works

hard.". Scarlet nodded with a forced smile pulling Violet

away back into the room.

"Tell me about your paradise Violet. How are all
your chickens?" She asked grinning ear to ear.

A Violet Night

Chapter 45.) *Epilogue*

A maid began to pass the silverware and dishes. Rory pulled a chair out for Violet and Rowan did the same for his sister. He patted his sons shoulder before motioning him to sit down as well. Lee also took his place at the table on the other side of Rory. Violet patted the maids arm "Never form a cross with your dishes at the table, it brings bad luck.". The maid looked at her curiously before rearranging the table. A woman entered the room with Scarlet they were gigging amongst themselves grabbing onto one another's arms.

A Violet Night

The woman had the deepest, richest, and most beautiful color of skin that would make even the nighttime sky jealous. The light in the room only illuminated her beauty. She had short black hair down to her scalp and big bright beautiful brown eyes. Rory looked at her oddly. Violet stepped on his foot harshly. The woman wore a white draping shirt cut open at the top tight enough to show her cleavage, and long white pants with a gold trim at the bottom with a silver sword hanging off her left hip. The handle was encrusted with emeralds.

"Everyone this is Amina." Scarlet nervously said letting go of Amina's arm. Violet smiled standing up to greet the woman. "So nice to meet you finally." She said with a thick foreign accent. While they were hugging she looked over her shoulder to her sister "Her?" She mouthed. Scarlet nodded her head with an ear-to-ear smile.

"Kids come meet Amina." Violet said to them motioning them to stand up. "Auntie Scarlet is Amina your girlfriend?" Lilliana asked hugging Amina. "She is actually my Fiancé." She corrected her niece still smiling greatly. "Really? She's so pretty!" She said looking up at the woman amazed. Rowen hugged her returning to his place at the table. Rory came up to her still in confusion. It wasn't uncommon for woman to love other women, but they are often kept hidden. "Don't make it weird Ri." Violet said watching him "It's okay Scarlet already warned me about you." She said flashing her bright white smile at him. Rory awkwardly put his arm out to shake her hand.

She met his hand with her own. "She is a crafted swordsman like you if not better Ri." Scarlet said proudly. "Maybe we could have a match sometime?" She said still smiling at him. She walked back over to Scarlet and gave her a kiss. "I think that would be hardly fair." He said to her with a smile. "Yes. To you it would be very unfair indeed." She said matching his tone.

A Violet Night

"Well I'm starving!" Rowan said loudly. "You're always hungry." Lilliana said rolling her eyes. Scarlet clapped her hands and the kitchen staff brought out the plates of food.

Rory looked at Scarlet and Amina laughing holding hands on the table with each other talking to Violet and the children. Rory with a straight face said, "When's the wedding?" loudly. He cracked his usually mischievous grin at them. They looked at each other in a state of euphoria. "Very soon." Scarlet said raising her glass to the sky. "Here's to very soon!" Rory said raising his glass. "Cheers to everlasting love and may I find it in this delicious food." Lee said digging into his plate.

A Violet Night

Dedications:

Tremendous thank you to David Lerch who always believed in my dreams and pushed me to be the best I could possibly be. Your words and teachings have stayed with me throughout the many years of perfecting my work. You taught me I could do anything I set my mind to, so I set out to do just that.

A Violet Night

Made in the USA
Columbia, SC
28 October 2022

70180284R00269